Redirecting Billy

JR THOMPSON

JR THOMPSON

REDIRECTING
BILLY

WORTHY BATTLE SERIES BOOK 2

Other Books By JR Thompson

Harmony Series
Hidden in Harmony: Danger is Imminent
Fighting for Farmington: Destruction is Inevitable
Terrors of Troy: Despair is Inflicted
Storms at Shelton: Deception is Inexcusable

Standalones:
Revenge Fires Back
Shady Valentine
Snowflakes To Iron

Worthy Battle Series:
Rebuilding Alden
Redirecting Billy
Reprogramming Carlos
Reforming Dawson
Renovating Elliot
Refurbishing Felipe (coming 2019)

Cover design by JR Thompson.

Discover more about Christian Author JR Thompson and his writings at www.jrthompsonbooks.com

All scriptures quoted and referenced in this book are taken from the Authorized King James Bible.

ISBN: 978-1-7337673-2-3

I am dedicating this book to William Burpee, a faithful reader who continuously encourages me to keep writing.

1

From his slightly less-than-cozy seat on the courthouse steps, the reddened eyes of fourteen-year-old Billy Andrews glued themselves to passing traffic. His momma wasn't playing when she ordered him out of the car. Still, he clutched a thread of hope. That woman loved him too much to leave him out on the streets, no matter what he had done.

"There she is," Billy mumbled as a smaller, tan-colored vehicle slowed. He started to rise before realizing it wasn't her. The hatchback had only reduced its speed to avoid plowing into a pedestrian.

With the sun beginning to set, Billy chewed his bottom lip. Where was he going to sleep? What would he have for dinner? She had to return; that's all there was to it. Leaning back, the teenager rested his elbows on the concrete step behind him. He wished he could cry but perfecting the art of emotional control for so many years had locked his tear ducts.

"Billy!" a man called from a nearby alley.

Recognizing the voice, the distraught teenager turned to see his probation officer motioning for him. Nervously, he descended the steps and met Mr. Bones on the sidewalk. "What you want, Mr. B? My momma send you here?"

"Your mother told me everything, Billy."

Billy put his hands in his pockets, "No surprise there. So, what now? You takin' me back to the crib?"

"Unfortunately, it doesn't sound like that's an option."

"Momma's serious?" Lifting his right foot, Billy stomped the sidewalk beneath him. "She ain't gonna let me come home?"

"Not right now, Billy. She's pretty upset."

"Fine then. She can be that way all she want to. So, where you shipping me off too? The runaway shelter or some group home?"

"Neither, Billy... You're coming to my place."

The young cupped his hand around his ear and tilted his head toward his probation officer, "Come again, Mr. B."

"I'm bringing you home with me... And it's Mr. Bones."

"That's cool," Billy said. "I can dig it." Billy convinced himself it was probably some kind of a game his momma was playing. Somehow, she had gotten Mr. Bones to go along with her. It was okay. He'd rather be with his probation officer than chillin' on those steps any day.

He followed Mr. Bones to the car. Inside, he received a firm lecture, "You and I have not yet had the opportunity to become well acquainted; I realize that. But that's going to change right now."

"What you mean?" Billy asked as the man started his car.

Pulling out, Mr. Bones replied, "To start with, we're going to go over some ground rules. There will be no profanity, alcohol, tobacco, drugs—"

2

"Weed ain't no problem, is it?"

"Billy, there you go with those double negatives again."

"What are these stupid double and triple negatives you keep griping about, Bones?"

"I'll give you a grammar lesson later. For now, let's stick to the guidelines you're going to adhere to. Yes, weed is a problem. You are not to smoke marijuana or—"

"You just talkin' 'bout in your crib or you meaning at school too?"

"Nowhere, Billy!"

"Understood... What else you got?"

"You will keep your pants on your waist, not around your knees."

That was taking things too far. "You can't expect me to change my style! This is who I am!"

Speaking in a forcedly calm voice, Mr. Bones said, "I expect you to comply with the rules. If you don't, you will be subjected to stiff consequences."

"What you gonna do if you catch me sagging?"

"I'm not getting into disciplinary actions right now; you should be ashamed of yourself for even asking about them. You just focus on doing what you're told."

Billy shook his head and gazed out the window. He did not like that man. Mr. Bones was a bully. Gonna sit there and give him a bunch of stupid rules. Try to force him to change his whole personality. Not willing to provide any explanations. Not going to tell him what kind of consequences to expect. There wasn't any excuse in that. None.

Mr. Bones continued, "You're to report to my office immediately after school every day."

Billy gave his probation officer an intense, penetrating stare. His nostrils flared as he said, "What?... Why?"

Echoing the words his own mother had bored into him when he was younger, the probation officer answered, "Because I said so. That's why."

As they stopped at a red-light, Billy reached for the radio. He swiftly drew his hand back upon receiving a death stare. Mr. Bones had control issues. Like it was gonna kill him if somebody turned on some music. It was too soon to make waves. Billy changed the subject, "How long we gonna be roomies, Mr. Bones?"

The light changed. Taking his foot off the brake, his probation officer replied, "Until we can convince your mother it's a good idea for you to return home."

Shaking his head, Billy retorted, "Like that's ever gonna happen!"

Mr. Bones ignored his remark and pulled into the parking lot of Clover Street Baptist Church just in time to see Ms. Moles wheeling across the pavement.

Billy stared at the elderly woman's wheelchair, glanced at the steeple, and took in the crowded parking lot, "I thought you was takin' me to your crib?"

"We'll be heading that direction after church."

"Church?" Billy wasn't having it. He didn't know what his momma was up to, but he wasn't about to become one of those soft, weak, Christians. "I ain't exactly the religious type, Mr. Bones... I'll wait in the car."

"Wrong! You will get out, pull those jeans up, tuck your shirt in, and accompany me inside."

What was that man's deal? Billy thought his momma knew how to nag. Mr. Bones was grating on his last nerve. "You be trippin', man!"

"Hurry up, Billy! Church is about to start, and I don't want to be late."

"I ain't had no dinner yet, sir... I'm hungry."

"I haven't eaten either."

Billy rubbed his stomach. In a whiny voice, he said, "Can't we just skip church tonight and get some take-out then?"

"Get out, Billy!"

With a sour expression on his face, Billy complied. Not only did he get out of the car, but he pulled his britches up and crammed the bottom of his polo into the waistband. "Let me guess; this is an all-white church, right? I'm gonna stick out like a hair in scrambled eggs!"

"Actually, Clover Baptist is extremely diverse. You'll fit right in."

"Me? I ain't gonna fit in at no church. No way. No how."

The probation officer chuckled, "Maybe not, but we're going in anyway."

2

Philip couldn't believe Billy would stoop so low the very first time he took the boy to church. Yes, he could have done worse. But did he have to open that fat mouth of his?

Billy reclined his end of the sofa. "What you keep crying 'bout this for?... Let it go already!"

"I can't do that, Billy. You need to understand that it's wrong to lie," Mr. Bones replied firmly.

"How you gonna look a brother in the eye and call him a liar?"

Pulling off his left loafer, Mr. Bones let it drop to the floor. "When you tell a bunch of teenagers you're in a gang even though you know good and well you aren't... that makes you a liar."

"Who died and made you judge? You don't know me! You ain't know nothin' about me! Ain't got no proof—"

"Okay then, gang-banga, why don't you convince me you're in a gang?" The probation officer kicked his other shoe on the floor. "What's the name of this gang you're affiliated with?"

Billy's face turned stone-cold as he said, "The Black Disciples."

Mr. Bones should have guessed. It never failed; every time one of his clients tried to convince him they were in a gang, it was always either The Black Disciples, The Bloods, or The Crypts. Working with real gang members on a regular basis made it quite simple to pick out the counterfeits. "Really?" he asked sarcastically. "And how long have you been living the gang life?"

Sipping his iced tea, Billy raised his eyebrows, "Since I was ten... What you gettin' all up in my business for?"

"Just trying to get the full picture, man. So how did you get inducted?"

"It's called an initiation," Billy scoffed. "They gave me a beat-down."

"Do me a favor and define beat-down for me."

Billy sat up straight, and a smirk appeared on his face. "You don't know nothing about gangs, do you, Mr. Bones?"

The probation officer was tiring of the teenager's cocky attitude. "Apparently I know more about gangs than you know about the English language."

"Oh, you feelin' another roast war? You so—"

"No, Billy. Let's not go there."

"You too afraid of losin'?"

Mr. Bones hadn't meant to exchange insults with the kid before. He wasn't about to get dragged into it again. His feelings for juveniles were difficult to explain. The rougher his clients were around the edges, the more he liked them. At the same time, there were a few who seemed to be experts at elevating his blood pressure — the young man sitting next to him was one such expert. "Just answer my question. Tell me about this beat-down you received."

Lowering his chin, Billy shook his head. He pulled his right foot atop his left knee, started to speak, but closed his mouth before anything came out. He sucked in a deep breath and then exhaled it loudly. Clearly miffed, he finally said, "I'm trying to be respectful here. Mr. Bones, I know you find certain words offensive... I can't rightly explain myself with these tight restrictions on my vocabulary."

Philip smirked. Buried somewhere beneath that tough exterior, Billy was a people-pleaser. It might take a while to excavate that part of his personality, but he was sure it existed. "I appreciate that," he said. "What did they do to you?"

Billy heavily dropped his foot back to the floor, "They beat me up. What you think they did?"

Philip gave him a once-over. The boy didn't have a single scar on his face. He was big-boned, but certainly not muscular. The hatred smeared across Billy's face was far from genuine. His story was becoming less believable by the second. "They beat you up when you were a ten-year-old little boy?" Mr. Bones asked.

"Yeah, man. Age don't mean nothing in the brotherhood. That's how they see if a guy has what it takes."

"Uh-huh," Mr. Bones said.

With the wildness returning to his eyes, Billy leaned forward. "You still don't believe me, do you?"

"No, Billy, I don't."

"Why's that?"

"We can talk about it another time, man. You've had a long day, and it's already going on 8:00."

"So?"

"You still need to get your shower, get those clothes washed, and get in bed by 10:30. "

"Whoa, whoa, whoa!" Billy kicked the footrest down and jumped up out of his seat. "You don't honestly expect me to go to bed at 10:30? I ain't in kindergarten no more, man."

"I'm *not* in kindergarten *any*more," Mr. Bones corrected him. "And have a seat."

"What? You think you're so high and mighty that you have the right to tell me when to stand and when to sit? You be trippin', Mr. B. I ain't no dog!"

"It's Mr. Bones and yes, sir. I did tell you to sit down, and you better do it right now!"

"Who you orderin' around like that?"

Mr. Bones lunged to his feet and charged toward the thug-wannabe. He didn't know what he was going to do if Billy challenged him but there was no way he was going to put up with any more of that lip. Somewhere along the line, Billy had gotten the impression that authority meant nothing. That was about to change — one way or another.

Fortunately, Billy was smart enough to sit down before his probation officer had to make a split-second decision regarding how far to take matters. "Look, man. I ain't mean to start no trouble. I can go to bed at 10:30; that's fine... but what's up with this whole laundry bit?"

"You're not going to school wearing dirty clothes tomorrow, Billy."

"I don't plan on it. Take me by my crib so I can get my stuff."

"Not gonna happen."

"Why?"

"Your decisions are what got you thrown out. You made your bed; it's time to lie in it."

"You trippin' if you think I'm gonna wear the same thing every day!"

Mr. Bones nodded with a mischievous smile. He had no intentions of allowing Billy to become a long-term house guest. Too comfortable of a nest might make the young man never want to leave. One way or another, he was going to inspire the fourteen-year-old to right his wrongs.

"That ain't okay, Mr. Bones! You got to get my stuff. I ain't about to be ruinin' my reputation over this."

"A gang member concerned about being in style? Impressive... You iron your t-shirts too, big boy?"

"Whatever, dude! So, how you expectin' me to clean my clothes? I ain't got nothin' to put on while they're in the wash."

Mr. Bones smirked. Billy might not have known it yet, but he had it made at home. Those luxuries were gone.

"Come on, man! This ain't funny!"

"Neither is what you did back at your place."

"What went on in my crib ain't none of your business."

"Yes, as a matter of fact, it is, Billy."

The teenager's eyes widened again, and his nostrils began to flare. "It was mine! It wasn't none of Momma's business what I did with it!"

"Then why did you call my cell afterward, saying you messed up and were scaring yourself?"

Billy shrugged his shoulders.

"What's that mean, Billy?

The fourteen-year-old slumped down on the sofa. "I wasn't thinking right when I called you. It was just a stupid mistake."

"Right, Billy... You keep telling yourself that. You know you were in your right mind when you phoned me. Right now is a different story altogether. You're just rattling off a bunch of nonsense."

"Excuse me? I ain't the one blowin' smoke out both sides of my mouth. You the one—"

"We're not going to fight all night, Billy. We have plenty of time to discuss things. But right now, you're going to—"

"Who says you get to decide when a conversation's over?"

"I do," Mr. Bones growled. "It's time to wash those clothes."

"Nah, man," Billy said, with his voice suddenly taking on a higher pitch. "I ain't feelin' it."

"Suit yourself, kid. Until you follow orders, I won't be fixing you any more meals. You'll have to fend for yourself."

"You think that's gonna bother me?"

The probation officer laughed, "And you'll get nothing but water to drink. Don't even think about using my ice."

Billy chewed on his bottom lip.

"And your bedtime is dropping to 9:30."

"Man, I ain't gotta put up with this! I don't got to live here!"

"You'll do as you're told, or you'll pay the price, Billy."

Billy stared at the floor for a moment before mumbling something under his breath.

"What was that?" Mr. Bones asked.

"I said... I'll do my stinkin' laundry."

"Good choice," Mr. Bones replied. "There are some towels in the restroom. You can throw one around your waist while your clothes are in the machine."

"You don't have anything I can wear? Some sweats or something would work."

"I'm not going to make any bones about this, Billy. You got yourself into this predicament, and I'm not going to make things easy for you."

"Fine. Whatever," the teen grumbled.

3

Scattered papers and mounds of folders on Philip's desk served as evidence that it had been a hectic Monday — three court hearings, a new client intake, four check-ins, a petition to revoke a client's probation, and too many phone calls to count. Glancing at his watch, he wondered if Billy was going to show up after school.

Just as the thought crossed his mind, he heard footsteps coming down the hall. Cassie marched in without bothering to knock. "Good afternoon, Philip," she said in a very business-like manner.

Philip's face turned a slight shade of red. He secretly hoped she had decided to give him another chance. "Good afternoon to you," he said while attempting to look deep into her soul. Sometimes Cassie could be a hard person to read.

"How are things going with Alden?" she asked.

Philip smirked. This conversation was starting off a lot better than the ones where she was on one side of a closed door, and he was on the other. Perhaps she had finally come to her senses. "He's a work in progress. I'm just thankful I have the—"

Cassie cleared her throat, "I wasn't looking for a long explanation. I was simply being polite," she sneered before whipping a necklace out of her purse and tossing it on his desk. "I just came by to return this."

"I bought that for you, Cassie. It's not mine anymore."

"I don't want the cheap thing!"

Philip stood to his feet, "Cheap? I paid over $300 for that necklace!"

"Whoever sold it to you saw you coming," Cassie laughed. "Oh, well. I don't feel right holding onto it — especially now that I'm seeing Nathan."

Philip shook his head. "I'm sorry... What was that?"

"You heard me, Philip! I'm seeing a man who worships the ground I walk on. He doesn't keep me hidden in the shadows. He doesn't consider me the least of his priorities. He values our relationship."

The office phone rang. "Hold on just a second, Cassie."

"No problem," she said. "I'm used to hanging out on the back burner."

It was obvious Cassie hadn't reconsidered. She was still far too immature to understand the call on Philip's life. He only wished there was a way he could get her to open her eyes. Jealousy was an ugly thing. The girl wanted one-hundred percent of his undivided attention; that was too much to expect of anyone.

"Philip Bones speaking...," He should have checked the caller id. Of all people to call, why did it have to be him? "Hi Alden, I was just talking about you, man... Of course, I was saying good things. I'm proud of you, bud... Unfortunately, I can't swing by today... I have... uh...," Philip looked up at Cassie for a moment, "I have another obligation... Is everything okay?... Alright, bud. In that case, I'll give you a call later tonight. Will that work?... Alright. Talk to you later." Philip hung up. "Sorry about that, Cassie... So, you're seeing someone else? It's a little soon. Don't you think?"

"I believe that's for me to decide. But apparently, I'm not the only one seeing someone else."

Philip shook his head. "I'm still single, Cassie. To be honest, I've been hoping we could get back together."

His former girlfriend took a seat. "Do you really expect me to believe that, Philip? I just heard you tell Alden you couldn't swing by his place tonight due to another commitment. Do you doubt my intelligence? You're crazy about that kid. There's no way you would blow him off unless you have a hot date."

Philip chuckled.

"What's funny?" Cassie asked.

Philip shook his head while continuing to smile.

"What, Philip?"

"Cassie... I'm not seeing anyone else. I can assure you of that."

"Really? I'd love to hear about an obligation that's more important than your thirteen-year-old heathen."

Philip sat back down. He knew he didn't owe Cassie an explanation. They may have worked in the same building, but he had his clients, and she had hers. At the same time, if there was to be even the remotest possibility of a rekindled flame, he was going to have to communicate. "One of my clients got himself thrown out of his house," he said.

"Oh... I'm sorry to hear that. What do you have to do? Give him a ride to a shelter?"

"He's staying with me for a while."

"You're allowing a client to move in with you? Are you nuts?"

"Cassie, we've been through all of this before."

"Yes, we have. And I still don't understand your way of thinking. You're asking for a lawsuit. You can't let juvenile delinquents stay at your place. That's a conflict of interest if nothing else."

Philip smiled, "This decision is not up for debate. God has called me to help these young men any way that I can, and that's what I plan to do."

Cassie stood. Raising her voice, she said, "Well, I have to thank you, Philip, for confirming that I made the right choice! The whole time we were dating, your mentoring took first place to our relationship. Now that this new client becomes a part of your life... you're willing to push Alden away for him. I'll never understand you!" Cassie spun around and bolted out the door.

Philip followed behind her. "Cassie, wait!... Please... Can we talk about this?"

At the end of the hall, Philip was stunned to see Billy sitting in the waiting room and even more so to see the teen grin and flirtatiously wink at Cassie as she stormed past him.

"Be right back," Philip said, following her into the hall. "Cassie!... Can we be adults about this?"

"Looks like you have someone waiting! Better tend to him!"

Giving up, Philip turned and walked back to the lobby. "Somebody got burned," Billy said. "Can't believe you let your women talk to you like that, Mr. B."

Mr. Bones was ready to explode. It took concentrated effort not to snap. Those foolish words came from a kid who didn't know better. Mr. Bones only had to remind himself of that about a dozen times a day. "It's Mr. Bones, Billy."

"Right. That's what I said."

"Billy!" Mr. Bones nearly shouted.

"Sorry, sir."

"That's more like it." Mr. Bones tried to regain his composure. "How was school?"

"How would I know? I've been hanging out at the mall all day."

Mr. Bones was boiling. How was he supposed to stay cool, calm, and collected when the client he was bending over backward to help was making a mockery of the whole situation? "To my office, now!... And get those jeans up!"

Once they were both in the office, Mr. Bones slammed his door and stood nose to nose with Billy. "You violated your probation and the rules of my house. You cannot, under any circumstances, cut class. That is completely out of line!"

"Yes, sir."

"What I want to know is why, Billy. I drove you to school. I dropped you off at the front door. How hard would it have been just to go inside?"

"Nobody said it was hard, sir."

Oh, that boy! He had better count his lucky stars that he was a client and not the man's son. Mr. Bones had to stay within semi-professional boundaries, no matter what was going through his mind. "So, you didn't even go to one class?"

"No, sir... I went to all of them."

"Why would you... wait!... You what?"

"I went to all of them. I was just pulling your leg, Mr. Bones... You should learn to control that temper."

The probation officer shook his head. "Have a seat, Billy."

"Yes, sir."

Mr. Bones walked around to the other side of his desk, sat down, and stared intently at Billy for a second. As angry as he had been, he couldn't stay that way for long. Grinning, he said, "You got me, kid."

"Thanks, Mr. B... I mean, Mr. Bones."

"You know I'm gonna have to pay you back, right?"

"For having a little fun?"

"Oh, you're not the only one with a sense of humor. Just wait, man. You'll get yours."

4

Tamara didn't know what she wanted. Ever since Mr. Bones said they were coming over, she hadn't been able to do anything. Her heart was full of love for her son, but his endless drama was dragging her down. The time for their meeting had finally arrived.

"Thanks for agreeing to speak with us," the probation officer told her.

"No problem," Tamara replied. "Let's go in here and sit at the dining table." She turned her attention to Billy, "I'm assuming you have something to say to me?"

Billy answered in a whisper, "I'm sorry, Momma."

Tamara detested that word. It sounded good but coming from her son, it didn't mean a thing; it never did. As they all took their seats, she demanded an explanation, "You're sorry for what?"

"For everything, Momma. I understand why you kicked me out. I've learned my lesson. Can I come back home?"

That's what she thought — Billy's apology was a sham. Just a manipulation tactic to get what he wanted. Did the boy forget they had lived under the same roof for the past fourteen years? "You ain't gonna be sleeping in this house again 'til you figure out how to obey me."

"I will, Momma."

"Let's find out if you will... Tell me who you sold it to, son."

"Momma!... I done told you — I don't know the man's name!"

Tamara cocked her head and wagged her finger under Billy's nose. "You are using that tongue for deceit, boy! You didn't sell it to no stranger! Not something that belonged to your daddy! I know you better than that now!"

"Momma, how many times we gonna have this talk? Can't you just let it go?"

Tamara started to reply, but Mr. Bones interjected, "Billy, you better try that again. You don't speak to any adult that way and especially not your mother."

Tamara mouthed a silent, "Thank you" to the probation officer for standing up for her. She was tired of her son's rudeness. Even though it happened practically every day, she never got used to it.

"So, what?" Billy shouted. "Now ya'll think you're gonna double-team me?"

"Nobody's double-teaming anybody, Billy. But you *will* respect your mother."

Billy laid his head on the table. "Raise that head up," Mr. Bones ordered. "You look at your mother and tell her who you sold it to."

Billy looked up. "I already told her... I know it was a stupid thing to do, but I sold it to a complete stranger because I needed the money."

Tamara smacked the table with an open palm. "You needed money? You didn't need nothing. You wanted. You

19

lusted after. You couldn't be man enough to resist temptation. You sold something of sentimental value just to get a temporary high!"

"I'm sorry, Momma!... Really, I am."

"Not as sorry as I am, son. If you'd just tell me who you sold it to, I could try to buy it back." Tamara didn't know where her son got his stubbornness from. When he was determined to hold back information, he could do it like nobody else. Time and time again she had witnessed him lie for days or weeks at a time before she finally discovered the truth on her own. He could say he was sorry a thousand times, beg for forgiveness, insist he knew nothing more — and none of it would mean anything.

"Momma, I done spent the money I got for it. You ain't got another $150 laying around here."

"$150?" Tamara shook her head in disgust. "That's all you got out of your daddy's pocket watch?" She wanted to stretch her hands around Billy's throat and choke the life out of him. Where did that boy come up with such foolish ideas?

"$150 was a lot of money, Momma... That thing was old; it wasn't even ticking no more."

The prideful expression on her son's face made Tamara want to hurl. His ignorance was astounding. "Your daddy inherited that watch from your granddaddy who inherited it from your great-granddaddy. The last time I looked it up, it was worth $800. It's probably worth more than that by now."

Billy pushed himself away from the table. "Whoa, whoa, whoa! You mean to tell me that guy crooked me?... Oh, man! He better hope I ain't never run into him on the street somewhere."

Tamara's eyes nearly bulged out of her head. "Billy, you're getting mad at the wrong person. The buyer ain't the one to blame here — you are! Your daddy handed you that watch when he was laid up in that hospital bed. Right when he was speaking his last words. How could—"

"Momma, please don't remind me," Billy said. "I know I was wrong. I feel bad enough as it is."

"That man loved you, Billy. He loved me. He was the best husband and father—"

"Stop it, Momma! Please, stop it!"

Tamara's eyes swam in tears. "You couldn't think of nothing but the drugs! Ain't your daddy worth more than that to you?"

"Yes, Momma! But I don't need that ole watch to remind me of him. I think about Daddy every day."

Tamara shook her head. "I don't know what to do, Billy. I'm at a loss here. You disrespect me. You don't care nothing about your deceased father. And it's not just this one incident either. I directly asked if you had any weed in this house and what did you tell me?"

"I don't have any, Momma!... You can search my stuff."

Tamara felt her heart tearing to pieces. It was getting to the point that she didn't even know her own son anymore. She hated to respond to his last statement because she knew an explosion would certainly ensue. But if it were going to happen, she'd prefer it take place in front of the probation officer. "I already searched your room, Billy," she told him.

Billy stood up. "You did what?"

"I went through everything with a fine-toothed comb, son."

Billy slowly turned himself in a complete circle while covering his face. "Oh no you didn't!... Momma! Why would you go and do somethin' like that?"

"Would you like to tell Mr. Bones what I found in your room or would you rather I show it to him?"

The probation officer gave Billy an angry stare, "I suggest you tell me, boy. Did you bring illegal substances into this house?"

Billy walked into the living room for a minute before slowly returning to his seat, "Mr. Bones, I wasn't honest with her... I had some marijuana under my bed."

"And that's not all, Billy," Tamara scolded. "Is it?"

"No, ma'am... Momma, I know this looks really bad. But I'm sorry... I really am."

Mr. Bones interjected, "What else did she find, Billy?"

Billy glared at his momma. "How long were you in my room?"

"Long enough to find it all, son."

"Fine," Billy grumbled. "Had some chewing tobacco, a couple of bottles of beer, a crack pipe, a pair of brass knuckles... That's all I remember."

"Pretty much sums it up."

Mr. Bones and Tamara looked at each other for a moment. "Do you have anything on you now, Billy?" Mr. Bones asked.

"No, sir. Nothing."

"So you have no objections to letting me search you?"

Billy shook his head, "Do what you gotta do, man! I ain't got nothin' to hide."

"You better not be lying to me."

"I ain't, man. Here, look!" Billy flipped his pockets inside out. With the exception of a gum wrapper, they were empty.

Mr. Bones turned his attention to Tamara, "Where do you want to go from here?"

"I keep asking myself the same question," Tamara replied. "But right now, I think my boy needs a man in his life. A man

22

who will lay down the law. Mr. Bones, how long can he stay with you?"

Mr. Bones glanced at Billy and then back at Tamara, "He can stay as long as it takes — but Tamara, he's your son. He needs his mother."

"I know that." It wasn't that Tamara didn't want him. She feared Billy. She never knew what he might take or who he might take it from. Every time somebody knocked on the door, she expected to see her son standing there in handcuffs. Never having a moment's rest was taking a toll on her mental stability.

"We need to work on getting him back here with you," the probation officer told her.

"I agree," Tamara said. Her heart was so heavy it hurt. She now understood the old adage about parenting not being for sissies. "Billy and I need some time away from each other."

"But Momma!" Billy interrupted. "This man's makin' me go to bed at 10:30! He won't let me hang out with my friends after school. He won't even let me dress the way I want to."

For the first time in their meeting, Tamara smiled, "I'm glad to hear that, Billy... Mr. Bones, keep up the good work."

"Keep up the good work?... Momma!"

"Hey, I ain't got no problem with somebody makin' you keep your boxers covered up."

Billy could tell he wasn't going to win this battle. He changed the subject, "Momma, can I at least get some of my clothes while I'm here?"

Mr. Bones answered for her, "Absolutely not! I already told you no on that one. You're not going to play your mother and me against one another."

"Momma! Do you hear this man?... He be wantin' me to wear the same clothes every day and to wash 'em every night!"

23

Mr. Bones spoke in Tamara's place again. "Not only is that the way I want things, but that's the way things are going to be until you get your act together. You want your clothes? Straighten up so you can move back into your own house!"

5

Sporting a white bath towel, Billy folded the futon couch into a bed while grumbling, "Mr. Bones think he all high and mighty. Be gettin' kicks outta rulin' over teenagers. He'll regret it one of these days."

The dryer buzzed for several seconds. Billy headed down the hall, mumbling, "My momma would yell 'til my eardrums ruptured if I ran the washer and dryer for one outfit — especially one that ain't even dirty. What a waste of electric! Ole dude must have a bigger stack of papers than he has brains."

Grabbing his clothes, the fourteen-year-old grew even more agitated. "Did I seriously leave an ink pen in my pocket? Man, Mr. B.'s gonna be all up in my face." Ink stains were all over the dryer, and the only outfit he had to his name was splattered with blue specks. There would be no way of denying that one.

The house phone rang, and Billy darted toward the living room, clothes in hand. "I've got it!" Mr. Bones called from the master bedroom.

That didn't stop Billy from picking up the other phone. He pressed the mute button just to make sure no one could hear him breathing.

"Sorry for not calling you earlier, Alden," he heard Mr. Bones say.

"It's okay," Alden replied. "I figured you were busy. Is this a good time to talk?"

"Yeah, man. How are things going at the Wamboldt place? You and your grandma getting along okay?"

Billy scratched his head, wondering who his probation officer was talking to. He could tell it was a kid and suspected it was probably another client.

"We're doing good. She said I couldn't talk very long tonight so I need to keep this kind of short."

"Now Alden, you have no idea how proud I am to hear that. Your grandmother gave you directions, and you're trying to comply. Way to go, bud!"

Billy grinned. Whoever the kid was, he must be a brat. It was pretty pathetic that he had to be patted on the back for following one instruction he was given. Sounded like a pretty cool kid.

"Thanks... I have a project I'm working on for school, and I was wondering if maybe we could go to the island this weekend and you could help me with it?"

Strike that thought. The kid must be a nerd. Who calls their probation officer and asks him to help with school work? Definitely not a kid Billy had any desire to meet.

"Well, buddy, I'm honored that you called to ask, but I don't know if I can this weekend. I've missed church the past two Sunday mornings. I don't know if you remember or not, but God might be calling me to preach."

"I remember. I'm not trying to keep you out of church. But... we still had services on the island, remember?"

Billy raised his eyebrows. So, his probation officer took this Alden kid to an island somewhere, and they had their own personal church services together? Like that wasn't weird or anything!

"Yeah, we did," Mr. Bones agreed. "But the Bible says we're not to forsake the assembling of ourselves together. As a Christian, God expects me to be in church."

"Well," Alden said. "What if we just hang out at the island Friday night and come home Saturday?"

"I'd love to, man... but I have a lot going this week—"

"I'll bring my trunks... I'll even take you up on that challenge to see who can swim to the other side of the river the fastest."

Mr. Bones chuckled. "Alden, you're awesome. Do you know that?"

Billy couldn't make up his mind what to think of this conversation. He could tell his probation officer and Alden had a special bond. After giving it some thought, he knew who the kid was. The white momma's boy Mr. Bones had been mentoring before.

"Thanks, Mr. Bones," Alden said. "But can we go?"

"I might have to ask for a raincheck on that one, bud. You see, I have another client staying with me right now."

There was a silence. Billy was curious as to where their conversation was going to go. A hand firmly gripped his shoulder from behind. Hesitantly, Billy looked up to find Mr. Bones glaring at him. Mr. Bones continued gripping his shoulder. Alden asked, "Another client? Is it that Billy kid?"

A puzzled expression came to Billy's face.

"Yes, Alden. It's Billy. He's just here for a little while."

Billy wondered how Alden knew his name. What exactly had Mr. Bones told him? He didn't appreciate being talked about behind his back.

"That's not fair!" Alden fussed. "I asked you to adopt me. You said it wouldn't look right for a single man to take in a thirteen-year-old."

"Alden, I still feel that way, but there were extenuating circumstances."

"Like what?"

"I can't exactly share other clients' personal lives with you, bud. It's against the law."

"Well, since Billy's already living with you, can I move in too?"

"No, Alden. It doesn't work like that."

"You know what?... Forget you, Mr. Bones. I thought you liked me, but it's obvious you don't!" Alden hung up.

The probation officer squeezed Billy's shoulder a little harder than he had been. "Hang... the phone... up. We'll discuss this in the morning... I'm heading back to my room to call Alden back. Don't even think about eavesdropping like that again."

"Yes, sir... Sorry, Mr. Bones."

"Wait a minute... what's that all over your shirt?"

Billy lifted it up off the couch and pretended he hadn't noticed. "I don't know," he lied.

"Let me see it."

Billy handed it to him. He looked toward the TV while chewing on his bottom lip.

"Do the rest of your clothes look like this too?"

Billy nodded but intentionally avoided eye contact. "Your washing machine must have messed up, sir."

"Come in here with me and let's have a look-see."

The fourteen-year-old shook his head. "You probably ought to call Alden back. Fixing the washing machine can wait 'til morning."

"Now, Billy! Let's go."

Taking his grand time, Billy got up off of the couch and followed Mr. Bones to the laundry room. Mr. Bones opened the dryer. "Just what I thought! You didn't check your pockets, did you?"

"It was an accident, Mr. Bones."

"And you knew about it when I first asked you about the shirt, didn't you?"

"Yeah, man."

"Why did you lie to me?"

"I ain't lie 'bout nothin'!"

"Alright, Billy. We'll deal with this at another time. Get in there and get to bed. I don't have time for this right now."

Billy didn't have to be told twice. He returned to the living room and threw his blankets on the make-shift bed. "I've done it now," he muttered. "Oh well, a few more days of tearing up his appliances and interrupting his phone calls and he'll make Momma take me back!"

Grabbing the remote, Billy turned the TV on and flipped to a sports channel. Mr. Bones barged into the room with the phone up to his ear. "It's past 10:30, Billy. Turn it off and leave it off."

"I always be fallin' asleep with the TV on."

"Not here you don't. Turn it off, now!"

Billy shook his head as he hit the power button. "Fine. Good night, Mr. Bones and—," he raised his voice to a shout, "You hear that, Alden? It's late! You ought to be in bed!"

Mr. Bones rolled his eyes and made his way back to the master bedroom.

Billy tried to fall asleep, but he couldn't do it; not with bits and pieces of his probation officer's conversation filtering through the door. He got up and tip-toed to the kitchen. Opening a few cabinets, he was disappointed to find nothing but health foods — definitely not his cup of tea.

Checking the fridge, Billy again found himself frustrated. Now the freezer, on the other hand, that's where it was at! Green mint-chocolate ice cream. That would hit the spot!

Taking out the box, Billy started to look for a bowl but thought better of it. Borrowing a spoon from the dishwasher, he ate right out of the box. After about a dozen spoonfuls or so, he closed the container and put it back in the freezer. What Mr. Bones didn't know wouldn't hurt.

6

Parking across the street from Westview Middle School, Philip whispered a prayer, "Dear Heavenly Father, please give me the opportunity to speak with Alden while I'm here. I know I'll see him in my office Thursday, but I can tell he's pretty sore with me right now. If I cross paths with the kid, please help me smooth out the ruffled feathers. Thank you in advance! I pray this in Jesus's name, Amen."

The probation officer locked his car and headed across the street. Once inside, he met Mr. Ponderosa in the hallway.

"Good morning, Mr. Bones. Hear to check up on Alden?"

"Yes, sir. How's he doing?"

"Much better," the principal replied. "Until this morning, anyway."

"That doesn't sound good. What happened?"

"Nothing serious — not for Alden anyway," the principal chuckled. "He knocked a kid's books out of his arms as he was walking down the stairs."

Philip shook his head. "What was his excuse?"

"Claimed it was an accident, but five witnesses say otherwise… He's earned himself three days of after-school detention."

Philip felt guilty. Alden had been doing better until the day after he had let him down. He didn't want to take the blame for the kid's actions; Alden had a mind of his own. But he also knew Alden was a troubled teenager who could easily slip back into his rebellious stage. If that was going to happen, he wanted to make sure he had done everything in his power to prevent it. "Would it be okay if I had a word with him?"

"I wish you would, Mr. Bones. You've had a profound effect on that young man. I don't know how you do it, but somehow you have that kid's respect. I'll tell you what; why don't you head to the office and I'll get Alden for you?"

"Sounds like a plan."

Sooner or later Philip would learn to be more specific with his prayers. Yes, he was going to see Alden but not under the best of circumstances. Moseying down the hall, he glanced into classrooms as he walked. The things he saw were interesting: students whispering to one another behind their teacher's backs, a girl's cell phone getting confiscated, a soft-spoken man trying to regain control of a room full of unruly students. It made him wonder how learning in such an environment was even possible.

Arriving in the office, he noticed a handful of student volunteers doing everything from manning the phones to organizing paperwork. A couple of adults were hanging out in the back of the office joking around and appearing to have the time of their lives. Philip took a seat next to a boy who was whiter than a ghost. He could only assume the kid was sick.

Fourteen minutes passed before Mr. Ponderosa showed up with Alden. "Sorry for the delay," he said. "Alden was in the middle of a math test."

"Not a problem," Philip said. "Do you have a conference room available by any chance?"

"Sure, right this way."

Alden followed the two men in silence.

Mr. Ponderosa opened a door and flipped on a light switch. "Will this work?"

"Yes, sir," Philip replied. "I'll just need about ten minutes or so with him."

"Take as long as you'd like," Mr. Ponderosa said, leaving the room and shutting the door behind him.

Alden plopped himself down. "Who snitched on me?"

Mr. Bones hated that question. For whatever reason, ninety-nine percent of his clients considered snitching to be a far worse crime than anything else imaginable. They didn't care if someone was a thief, a bold-faced liar, or a drug addict. But a snitch didn't deserve to live. The twisted logic of teenagers was worrisome. Regardless, Mr. Bones was glad he could honestly say no one had called to report the boy's misdeeds.

Alden ran his fingers through his hair as he looked down at the table. "Of course, you'd come by on the one day I get sent to the office."

"Purely a coincidence, Alden... What happened today?"

"Same ole, same ole. Always getting blamed for things I didn't do."

"Alden, your principal says he's seen significant improvement in your behavior lately... Don't mess up now... Do you remember our conversations about how we have to teach our mouths what they can and can't say?"

Alden nodded.

"Don't let your tongue win a victory. That thing wants to lie. You teach it to obey you. You're an honest young man who is trying to improve his reputation. Don't let that mouth ruin it for you."

Alden balled both fists, released them, and slowly stretched out his fingers.

"Same thing applies to that temper, buddy. You are in control of your anger; it doesn't rule you anymore. Remember?"

The thirteen-year-old took a deep breath. "Okay... You're right — I can do this. I'm not mad, and I'm not going to lie. I knocked Eric's books down the steps... I didn't do it to be mean. I was just trying to give everybody a laugh."

"So, you've reverted back to bullying? I thought you got all of that out of your system, man?"

Alden crossed his arms and mumbled, "That's what you get for thinking."

It had been a while since Alden had spoken to Mr. Bones in such a disrespectful manner. He was right; Alden was upset with him. "Are you jealous?"

"Jealous?" Alden sounded shocked that his probation officer would even suggest such a thing. "What do I have to be jealous of?"

"I don't know... Billy moving in with me maybe?"

"Why would that upset me?... I mean... just because you let him stay with you even though I asked first doesn't phase me at all."

Mr. Bones shook his head. The last thing he ever wanted to do was hurt Alden. He had come so far. It would be a shame to see all of that progress go down the toilet. "Alden, we've been through this. You have a grandmother who loves you. You need to be with your family."

"And Billy doesn't need to be with his?"

"Billy should be with his family as well; we're working on that."

"Right," Alden said sarcastically.

"Listen, I'm hoping to have Billy back at his place no later than the end of this weekend. If he's still with me Friday... what do you say we talk to your grandma about you coming over and spending the night with us? That way you guys can get to know each other, and you and I can spend some time talking or whatever."

Alden fought to keep a straight face. "I guess I can do that... if you really want me to."

"I would love to have you over, Alden... However, if you get into any more trouble at school, this weekend is off. Understand me?"

"Yes, sir."

"Now, I want you to apologize to Mr. Ponderosa and to Eric. Not just a quick 'I'm sorry,' but a sincere, heartfelt apology. Do I make myself clear?"

"Yes, sir."

7

Toward the end of the Wednesday evening prayer service, Philip's breathing shallowed, his heart began to race, and there was no doubt about it — the Holy Spirit was at work. Philip couldn't stay in his pew any longer. Nearly sprinting his way to the altar, tears streamed down his cheeks. On bended knees, he prayed silently in his heart, *Precious Heavenly Father, oh... thank you so much for making it clear to me. Yes, Lord, I'm willing. I would love to preach the gospel! Yes, it scares me to death. But I surrender my life to Your will and service. I'll do whatever You want me to do. I'll go wherever You want me to. You give the orders, and I'll follow them.*

A hand fell on Philip's back. He glanced up to see Pastor Jahmal. "Everything okay, Brother?"

Philip leaned over and hugged him. "Pastor, your message hit home tonight! God has been dealing with me for weeks, but I wasn't sure until tonight... He wants me to be a preacher!"

Pastor Jahmal chuckled. Jumping up, he shouted, "Praise belongs to the sweet Almighty Lord Jesus! Can I get a witness?"

Clover Street Baptist Church erupted in shouts of "Well, glory!... Praise His Holy Name!... He is worthy!... You got that right, Pastor!"

When things calmed down, a gentleman in the back said, "Pastor... what exactly are we praising Him for?"

Pastor Jahmal laughed, "Sorry about that, folks! I guess I got caught up in the moment." He placed an arm around Philip. "The Lord just used our church to birth a new preacher-boy! Everybody come up here and shake this man's hand!"

Philip was bubbling over with joy as folks lined up to share their words of encouragement. He couldn't remember ever having such a tremendous peace in his soul. Other than teens he had mentored, Philip had never taught anyone from the Word of God — but that was about to change.

"Brother Philip," Pastor Jahmal said. "One thing I've learned throughout my years of ministering is that a man doesn't learn to swim until he gets thrown into the water. Sunday evening, you're going to fill this pulpit."

Philip tensed up. "This Sunday? Like, in four days, Pastor?"

"Yes, sir. I want you to memorize and apply II Timothy 4:2 to your life, son. It says to, 'Preach the word; be instant in season, out of season; reprove, rebuke, exhort with all longsuffering and doctrine.' There's no better way to put that scripture into practice than just to get right in there and preach! You can do it, brother!"

Philip chuckled nervously. He was glad somebody had confidence in him. If it were his decision, he wouldn't preach his first sermon without taking at least a month to prepare.

Billy strutted up to the altar and gave his probation officer a fist bump, "When Momma finds out I'm livin' with a preacher, she ain't never gonna let me move back home. We ain't gonna tell her 'bout this, right, Mr. Bones?"

37

"We're not keeping any secrets from your mother."

"Figured as much," Billy mumbled before moving on so the rest of the congregation could congratulate him.

For another ten minutes, Philip shook hand after hand. He smiled so long he feared his face was going to get stuck that way. Eventually, the swarm dispersed and he and Billy were free to head to the house.

"Do you think you know enough about the Bible to preach to that crowd?" Billy asked.

"I hope so," Mr. Bones chuckled.

"If I were you, I'd be terrified of preaching to Pastor Jahmal. How long's he been pastoring? Like twenty years?"

"Twenty-three," Mr. Bones said.

"Wow! That ain't intimidating or nothin'."

"That *isn't* intimidating or *anything*," Mr. Bones corrected.

"Yeah, yeah... So, when are you going to find time to study? I mean, you work all day, and we keep pretty busy in the evenings."

"I'll figure it out, Billy."

"If it were me, I'd want to practice somewhere. You have someplace you wanna go after work tomorrow? I could stay at the house to give you some space."

Mr. Bones shook his head. "Nice try, pal. I'm not buying it."

"Buying what?"

"Whatever it is you're trying to sell me."

The drive home seemed to take forever — mostly because Billy did everything he could to make his probation officer more nervous than he already was. But that was okay — Mr. Bones had a plan. As soon as they walked in the door, he ordered Billy to get his clothes in the wash.

"What's the rush? It's only 8:30."

"Hurry up. We have things to do, Billy."

"Like what?"

"Just do as you're told, and you'll find out."

"Better not be something stupid, Mr. B. I'm tired."

"It's Mr. Bones."

"You don't think I know that?"

"If you know it, say it. I'm getting tired of repeating myself."

"Yes, sir."

Mr. Bones sat down in the living room and flipped his Bible open. A few minutes later, Billy returned wearing his towel. "Have a seat," Mr. Bones said.

"Am I in trouble?"

"No, sir. But I decided to take your advice."

"What advice was that?"

"You said I should find a place to practice before I preach Sunday evening. Congratulations, man. You get to be my audience."

Billy shook his head. "Nah, man. That's okay. I meant you could practice by yourself somewhere."

"Oh, no," Mr. Bones replied. "When I preach in church, people are going to be sitting out there in front of me. I can't very well practice without somebody listening."

"Fine," Billy said. "I'll sit here. But do I really have to listen?"

"You most certainly do... Here's a Bible. Turn to Isaiah 5:20. I'm not going to preach the full sermon. Just a small snippet of it — a part I believe you'll be able to relate to."

"Isaiah? Where's that?" Billy asked while flipping pages.

"In the Old Testament, man."

Billy shuffled through his Bible for another thirty seconds or so before saying, "I've got it... What chapter?"

"Chapter five, verse twenty."

Billy turned a few more pages. "I'm here. Let's get this over with."

Mr. Bones stood up and held his Bible in front of him. "The Word of the Lord says 'Woe unto them that call evil good, and good evil; that put darkness for light, and light for darkness; that put bitter for sweet, and sweet for bitter!' Church, our nation has completely turned itself upside down. We have people out there, brothers and sisters in Christ even, who believe success is measured by a person's wealth in spite of the fact the Bible declares the love of money to be the root of all evil!

"There are well-bodied souls right here in this community who brag about cheating our government by getting compensated for disabilities they don't have. Brothers and sisters, this passage of scripture says those people better be careful. If something is dark, it's from the devil himself and a Christian ought to stay as far away from it as he can. He shouldn't be okay with sin. He ought to detest it. He ought to run from it. He ought never to be associated with it."

Mr. Bones was raising his voice and having a grand time. Billy smiled. He didn't know Mr. Bones had it in him. "Amen, preacher! You tell it!" he shouted.

Mr. Bones smiled and continued, "And church, let me tell you this; No man, woman, boy, or girl sitting under my voice tonight ought to pretend to be something they're not — especially when that something doesn't align itself with scripture. Why young people like to pretend they're sexually active when they ought to be proud of their virginity is beyond me."

Billy shook his head in disbelief.

Mr. Bones ignored him. "Why kids act like they're not smart enough to get good grades just to impress the popular crowd is detestable. And should I even mention the young men out there who try to make people think they're involved in gangs? What is this world coming to? Woe unto them that call evil good and good evil—"

Billy held a hand up, "Stop, Mr. Bones. I ain't wantin' to hear no more of this."

The probation officer closed his Bible. "Of what, Billy?"

"Of you lecturin' me about the whole gang thing. You still don't believe me, do you?"

"Billy, you're not a member of any gang."

"Bet!"

"What?"

"How much you wanna bet? You can ask my momma. She'll tell you I'm in a gang."

If Mr. Bones had a quarter for every time he heard that line! When a person felt the need to bring up a witness to vouch for their story... it most always meant the same thing — their story was nothing more than a fable. "Your momma will tell me that, huh?"

Billy nodded.

"I could call her up on the phone right now, and she'd say you're a member of The Black Disciples?"

"You better believe it."

Mr. Bones whipped out his cell phone and dialed Tamara's number. There was only one way to find out!

Billy shook his head and silently gave Mr. Bones a look that said, "You're making a fool of yourself."

Mr. Bones could only hope calling the boy's bluff would work out in his favor. "Hi, Tamara, this is Philip Bones. I'm going to put you on speaker phone, is that okay?"

"Sure. No problem."

"Thanks!... I've got your son sitting here with me, and he says you'll vouch for him that he's a gang member."

Tamara laughed sarcastically, "What?... Billy, can you hear me right now?"

"Yeah, Momma. Will you tell this man I'm a Black Disciple?"

"Well, I could... but I'd be lying through my teeth."

"Momma! You know it's true!"

"Billy, why you always goin' around playin' make-believe like that? Ain't nobody in their right mind believe you in a gang."

"What you talkin' about Momma? You know the truth. Tell it like it is."

"Oh, I'll tell it alright. Billy, you ain't man enough to be in no gang. What would The Black Disciples want with you? How would you benefit them? They'd see you as a crybaby, boy. They wouldn't trust you. You ain't got nothin' they want."

"Momma!..." Billy was irate. "You know what, Mr. B? Just hang up the phone. We don't need to sit here listenin' to all these lies."

"Boy, don't make me come over there!" Tamara shouted.

"Tamara," Mr. Bones said, "I'm sorry for upsetting you—"

"Oh, you're not the one who upset me. It's that low-life sitting there with you!"

"Tamara, why don't we go ahead and end this call so I can deal with Billy?"

"I'll let you deal with him under one condition."

"What's that?"

"That you promise to beat the fire out of him!"

Mr. Bones chuckled. He couldn't deny feeling like the teen deserved a good thrashing but—

"This man ain't gonna touch me, Momma!" Billy yelled.

It wasn't his place. Mr. Bones didn't have it in him. "He's right, Tamara. I'm not going to beat him. I have other ways of getting my point across."

"I sure hope so. Heaven help that child!"

"That's his biggest hope, ma'am. Giving his life to Jesus."

"I've heard Jesus can work miracles. I'd love to see one in Billy's life. While we're waiting for that to happen though, you have my permission to do whatever it takes to get that boy of mine in line; I mean it."

"I understand, Tamara. I'll do my best with him. You have my word on that."

8

Unlike the vast majority of his peers, Billy wasn't upset by having to sit right in front of his Social Studies teacher — especially considering the fact that Ms. Galloway kept herself so engrossed in romance books that he could get away with anything.

Watching her facial expression for a moment, Billy could tell it was a safe time to make his move. The fourteen-year-old deviously eased his hand forward and snatched her black permanent marker. John, the kid sitting next to him, gave him a thumbs-up and a crooked smile.

Billy pushed the marker into his pocket and kept it there until break time. With the halls full of chaos, the teen leaned his back against a bulletin board and took out the marker. He glanced around; nobody was paying a lick of attention to him. Taking the cap off, he brought the tip up to his nose. It was strong, but boy did he ever love that smell! A few more long drawls like that, and he'd at least be able to get a little high.

In no time, Billy forgot all of life's pressures and felt like he was on top of the world — until Patrick, the biggest tattler in the school, happened by. "What are you doing?"

Billy jumped toward him, and the boy flinched. "You say a word to anybody, and I'll snap your neck."

Nearly trembling, Patrick said, "I won't say anything... I promise."

"You better be a man of your word."

"I am. You can trust me... Do I look like somebody who would double-cross you?"

Billy chuckled, "Nah, man. I reckon not."

It wasn't long before the bell rang. Billy slipped the marker back in his pocket and headed to fourth period. He didn't make it ten feet before the principal caught up to him. "Empty your pockets, Mr. Andrews."

"Empty my pockets? Why?"

"Now, please."

Billy looked around him. None of the other students were being harassed. They were getting in and out of lockers, cutting up with their buddies, or heading into classrooms. Of course, he would be the one singled out. "Why? 'Cause I'm black?"

Mrs. Hendricks put her hands on her hips, "That won't work with me, mister! I'm just as black as you are."

"Bein' blessed with dark skin don't mean you black. You just a giant snowflake that fell into in a black woman's body!"

"Excuse me?" Mrs. Hendricks said, cocking her head. "What is that supposed to mean?"

Billy could tell he had the upper hand. She was going into defense mode. If she wanted to make a scene, he was going to be the star. Mocking her, he put his hands on his hips and made an ugly face. In a whiny voice, he repeated her question, "What is that supposed to mean?"

Mrs. Hendricks started to speak, but Billy cut her off, "The way you talk, how you be carryin' yourself all up in here like you be somethin' special... you call that black?"

"Boy, you wouldn't know what black was if it smacked you upside the head. Black isn't dressing like a thug, using poor grammar, having no education, or being locked up in a prison cell."

"At least I'm real. It's a lot more than anybody could say for you!"

"I am legit, Mr. Andrews. I am not putting on airs. Like me or hate me, I am who I am."

"And so am I."

"Billy, I see what you're doing here — you're stalling. Empty those pockets."

Billy didn't move. He just stared her down. That old woman could flap her gums all she wanted to, but she couldn't make him do anything. She was short, weak, and scared. Oh, she was trying not to show it alright — but on the inside, she was shaking like a leaf.

Mrs. Hendricks took a step backward. "Would you prefer I call the school resource officer?"

"I ain't afraid of no officer," Billy said, "but seein' as to how you 'bout to make me late for Spanish, here!" Pulling the marker out of his pocket, he said, "I'm assuming this is what you want?"

"Exactly!... Let's go," she snapped, heading down the hall toward her office. "Where'd it come from?"

"Found it."

"Why do I find that story hard to believe, Mr. Andrews?"

"I don't know," Billy said. "You got trust issues, maybe?"

"Hmm," Mrs. Hendricks said as they entered her office, "I guess I'm going to call your mother."

"My momma ain't gonna care that I found a dollar store marker and put the thing in my pocket."

"She won't care that you were getting high off of it?"

"Getting high?... Is that what you do with your markers, Mrs. Hendricks? I ain't like that."

"Billy, I saw you!"

"You saw me doing what?"

"Holding that marker up to your nose. Your eyes are even red. Look in the mirror."

"I ain't gonna look in no mirror. You and your ugly face probably done broke the thing anyhow."

"Billy, I'm calling your mom."

"Because I was looking at a marker? Do you know how immature you sound right now?"

"Immature?... Billy, give me a break! Why do you want to kill your brain cells like that?"

"I wasn't killing no brain cells. I was looking at a marker!"

"With your nose?"

"I was tryin' to see if anybody had their name written on it so I could return it to them."

"Good one," Mrs. Hendricks laughed. "What's your mom's number?"

"I ain't giving it to you."

"Have it your way, Billy." Mrs. Hendricks logged into her computer and pulled up the number within minutes. "Good afternoon, this is Lakeisha Hendricks at the high school... Ms. Andrews, I just caught Billy getting high off of a marker he stole... I don't know yet... I will have to check with the school resource officer to see if he wants to press charges... He sure is. Would you like to speak with him for a moment?... Sure, hold on."

Billy glared at his principal while picking up the receiver. He wished Mrs. Hendricks wasn't sitting right there. It didn't matter. It's not like he cared what she thought anyway. "The woman's lyin' 'bout me, Momma! I wasn't getting high, and I ain't steal nobody's marker!"

"You listen to me, Billy Andrews, and you listen good! I have had it up to my eyeballs with your stealin' and lyin'. If that school presses charges against you, don't expect me to hire a lawyer. You can get one of those worthless public defenders to represent your behind, and if you end up in juvie, I couldn't care less."

Billy noticed a smirk on his principal's face. His mother had been so loud, he was certain Mrs. Hendricks had heard every word. "Momma, how you gonna take her side? You don't even know this woman!"

"But I know you, baby. I'm gonna get off of here and phone your probation officer. What you think he gonna say 'bout all of this?"

This thing was getting blown way out of proportion. First his principal, then his momma, and now his probation officer. What next? Was somebody going to inform the president of the United States? "Momma, please don't tell him!"

"Why?"

"Cause... Well, Momma...," Billy stumbled to find his words. "Mr. Bones is all excited. He got called to preach last night at church and—"

"He did?... That's wonderful, Billy. But why on earth would that stop me from tellin' him about your behavior?"

"Cause you wouldn't want to steal the man's joy, Momma! He's gonna preach his first sermon Sunday night. He got some serious studyin' to do. Worrying about some piddly little thing like a marker I found ain't gonna make things easier for him, Momma. Know what I'm sayin'?"

"Oh, I hear you loud and clear. You afraid of what that man might do to you, aren't you, boy? Mr. Bones must be a better disciplinarian than I am, huh? You always did respond better to male authority figures. And now you're stayin' with a preacher. Can't get no better than that. You better believe I'm gonna call him. I hope he blisters you!"

Billy lifted his eyes to meet those of Mrs. Hendricks. She looked like she was struggling to keep a huge smile off of her face. Billy couldn't believe the words flying out of his momma's mouth. He would have expected it if they were face-to-face in the privacy of their own home. But he was at school, and his momma knew he was sitting there with his principal. Had the woman no shame? Billy lowered his voice a notch, "He ain't like that, Momma."

"Oh, he might not be... yet! That's just 'cause he ain't been parenting very long. You just give the man time... And give me the opportunity to do some convincing."

Billy could only hope he was right about Mr. Bones. He knew his momma could be pretty persuasive, but his probation officer seemed like the kind of guy who did things his own way. Still, Billy didn't want to take any chances. "Momma, please don't tell him 'bout this. I'm beggin' you!"

"Beg all you want to. I'm callin' the man. Let me talk to your principal."

"Yes, ma'am."

Billy handed the phone back to Mrs. Hendricks, "She wants to talk to you."

"This is Mrs. Hendricks... No problem, ma'am... Yes, I think that's a fine idea... Sounds like Billy has some respect for him... Sure... As a matter of fact, why don't you tell his probation officer he's more than welcome to stop by anytime?... You too. Take care."

Hanging up the phone, Mrs. Hendricks gave Billy a look that said, "You've had it now." However, she didn't say a word.

"Well?" Billy asked.

"Well... are you going to level with me?"

"Let's see here. How'd you put it a few minutes ago? You wouldn't know the truth if it smacked you upside that ugly mole stickin' out your neck!"

"Billy, you are getting yourself in deeper water than you're going to be able to swim out of. You need to watch the way you speak to people. You wouldn't be in this mess had you simply kept your nose clean. You know we have a zero-tolerance policy for drugs in this school!"

"Drugs?... It's a marker, not crack!"

"But you used it to get high, Billy!"

"I did no such thing! But even if I did, why would you care? Can you honestly tell me you ain't never done it?"

"I can tell you that. Not once in my life have I ever sniffed a marker."

That was an interesting response. Billy couldn't help but notice how specific she was with her answer. "But have you gotten high?" he asked.

"Billy... I'm not perfect."

The fourteen-year-old smiled. He had the woman right where he wanted her, "So, I'll take that as a yes."

Mrs. Hendricks sighed. "I don't know if I should tell you this, but yes, Billy, in my earlier years, I did get high from time to time... but that's not something I'm proud of."

"Maybe not but look at you now. It didn't hurt you, Mrs. Hendricks. You're sitting here raking in the big bucks."

Mrs. Hendricks took a deep breath. "Billy, I had to work for what I have. I had to give up the drugs and chase after my dream. I went back to school and earned my G.E.D.—"

Billy chuckled sarcastically. "Your G.E.D.? You dropped out of school and think you got room to criticize me?"

"I'm not criticizing anybody, Billy. I'm trying to get you to understand."

"Understand what?"

"That you are an American citizen and as such your future can be whatever you want it to be."

"I ain't gonna amount to nothing, Mrs. Hendricks. I ain't like you. Can't afford no college. Tired of school anyway. Ain't about to get no fancy degree."

"Why, Billy? You don't have to have money to go to college. There are scholarships all over the place... Don't you have any dreams? Anything you want to accomplish in your life?"

"I'll probably be dead before I'm eighteen. Who cares about the future?"

"Young man, will you please listen to me?"

"I'm all ears," Billy replied.

"You can be anything — a firefighter, a police officer, a doctor, a lawyer, a mayor, a governor, the—"

Billy chuckled. He hoped the woman didn't truly expect him to buy into all of that. "You're funny," he said. "How many times a day do you give this speech?"

"I give it a lot, Billy. I'm not going to lie about that. But I give it because it's true. I can't stand to see young people drown themselves in sewage. Please, Billy. Please examine yourself. Please climb out of the sludge."

Billy shook his head. "Are you finished?"

Mrs. Hendricks sighed again. "Yes, Billy. I am."

"Can I go back to class now or is my momma comin' to pick me up?"

"For now, you can go back to class. I'm waiting to hear from your probation officer before I make a final decision as to your consequences."

"What does my probation officer have to do with anything? He ain't in charge of the school."

"No, Billy, he isn't. But I would like to speak with him anyway."

9

Rose tapped on Philip's door, "Miss Abby Gainsworth is here to check-in."

Covering the phone receiver, Philip told his secretary to send the girl back. As Rose left the room, he continued his call, "Yes, ma'am. Unfortunately, I have some clients scheduled to come in today. Otherwise, I would be there in a heartbeat... Billy's supposed to stop by my office after school today; I'll deal with him then... Yes, ma'am... I appreciate it... Feel free to call me anytime. Okay?... Alright. Enjoy the rest of your day."

Abby ambled in alone and closed the door behind her. "Both of your foster parents have to work this afternoon?" Mr. Bones asked.

"Yeah. That's what they said to tell you anyway."

"Abby, you know how to address adults. Never just say 'yeah.' Try 'yes, sir'; you'll earn people's respect."

"Mr. Bones, have you ever heard me say, 'Yes, sir?'... I'll answer that question for you... no, you haven't. I haven't said it, and I'm not going to. Believe it or not, we still live in America and our right to free speech has yet to be taken away."

Mr. Bones picked a pen up off his desk and rolled it between his hands.

Abby wasn't finished. "Um… do you know that music you're playing is Christian?"

"Yes, I do."

"I find that offensive. The court system says I have to come in here and see you. It doesn't say you have the right to cram your religious beliefs down my throat. I don't believe in God, and I don't want to hear that garbage. You gonna turn it off or am I going to do it for you?"

Mr. Bones shook his head. Meetings with Abby were always interesting. The girl's middle name should have been Drama. Even though Mr. Bones tried to make his clients semi-comfortable, he did not cater to bullies. "Isn't that interesting?" he asked. "A moment ago, you were telling me about the freedoms we have here in America. Why is it that you have the freedom of expression and I don't? Why is it so offensive for me to play the kind of music I enjoy while working in my own office?"

"Because you're a government employee and there is a separation of church and state."

"The First Amendment, Miss Abby, was written to ensure the government did not interfere in church-related affairs. It has absolutely nothing to do with a Christian's right to listen to gospel music or to share the Word of God with others. However, unlike some of the clients who come into my office, I do care about the feelings of others. I am not so addicted to my music that I can't turn it off when the need arises. Why don't you try asking me nicely?"

"Sure," Abby scoffed. "I'll be as nice as I know how to be… Turn that stupid thing off before I throw it out the window, *please*."

Mr. Bones smirked, "Ah, now that's better," he said. "Sorry, Abby. The radio stays on for this session. You touch it, and you'll earn yourself an all-expenses-paid vacation to juvie. I will not think twice about pressing charges... From what I'm seeing and hearing this afternoon, my guess would be things haven't improved any, right?"

"The Talbots gave their notice. We're waiting for the agency to find a new placement. They're dragging their feet like always, probably hoping the Talbots will change their minds."

"You've been through, what, five foster homes during the last year? When are you going to get it, Abby? No one is going to put up with a smart-mouth. You need to learn some manners."

"It's not like I care about any of those foster families anyway! I just want to be an adult so I can move out on my own."

Mr. Bones chuckled. Teenagers and their blindness to reality! If only she had a clue what the adult world was all about.

"I didn't say anything funny," Abby growled.

"I didn't mean to laugh," Mr. Bones replied. "But the truth is, with that attitude, you're never going to hold down a job. How do you plan to pay your rent?"

"My rent?" Abby scoffed. "I'm going to buy a house as soon as I turn eighteen."

Was there anything that girl didn't have an answer for? What kind of dream-world was she living in? Even though he had failed at reaching her on multiple occasions, Mr. Bones decided to try again, "How much money do you have saved up?"

"That's personal."

"Nothing... Just as I suspected," Mr. Bones replied.

Abby glared at him without saying a word.

"Let's move on," Mr. Bones told her. "How are things going at school?"

"Got my report card yesterday. One C and the rest were F's. What's that tell ya?"

"That you need to get it together and fast. You are smart enough to achieve better grades than that."

"I'm gonna drop out as soon as I'm old enough, Mr. Bones. It doesn't matter."

The probation officer's appointment with Abby seemed to soar into eternity. Month after month he tried to talk some sense into her, but she wasn't going to learn anything until she hit rock bottom. It was heartbreaking. So much so, as a matter of fact, that Mr. Bones breathed a sigh of relief when she finally left his office.

For once, he was relieved to be meeting with a new client. Speaking with anyone else would be a breath of fresh air after that! Stepping into the lobby, he introduced himself to the scrawny, nervous teen. "Carlos?... "My name's Mr. Bones... Is this your father?"

"Yes."

"That's yes, sir," Mr. Bones corrected him.

Truly sounding apologetic, Carlos replied, "Yes, sir... Sorry, sir."

Mr. Bones turned to his client's father, "Nice to meet you, Mr. Estrada."

"The pleasure is mine," Mr. Estrada said in a voice so quiet it was nearly inaudible.

"If you gentlemen wouldn't mind, please follow me back to my office."

Mr. Bones wasted no time in getting down to business. "Initial meetings like this one generally take about an hour. To be honest, I have a lot going on today; I'm going to see if we can speed things up a bit. Hope that's okay with you fellas."

"Not a problem," Mr. Estrada said.

"How about you, Carlos? Do you mind if we rush through this?"

"No, sir. Not at all."

"Great. Carlos, I've got your file in front of me; looks like you're here because you got caught sending inappropriate photos of yourself to a couple of girls at school. Tell me about that."

The thirteen-year-old's face colored, "I don't know what to say."

Mr. Bones leaned forward in his chair. "There's no reason to be shy now, Carlos. If you can share indecent pictures of yourself, there's no reason you can't talk about what you sent."

Mr. Estrada looked down at the floor, obviously as uncomfortable as his son was.

"I... uh..."

Mr. Bones didn't have time to play around. He would never understand why people always wanted to delay embarrassing answers. It wasn't like that was going to ease any humiliation they felt. It was going to be said one way or another. "Come on, Carlos. Spit it out! We can't speed up this meeting if you keep stammering around... What kind of pictures did you send?"

Carlos looked as if he could cry. "Bad ones, okay?"

"How bad?"

"Do I seriously have to tell you this? Isn't it in my report?"

"It is. But I always ask my clients to tell me exactly what transpired just in case something in my file was reported inaccurately. Tell me about these photos."

Carlos twiddled his thumbs nervously, "It was just two pictures."

"What were they of?"

The boy took a deep breath. "Of me... with no clothes on."

"Full-body shots or of something specific?"

"Full-body."

"And how did you manage to get full-body photos of yourself? Did you take the pictures or did someone else take them for you?"

"I took them myself, using the bathroom mirror."

Mr. Bones wasn't surprised. If he could only get a message out to the world warning of the dangers of modern-day electronics. If he had his way, it would be illegal for teens to have cell phones. They made it far too easy for young people to explore their sexual curiosities and get themselves in trouble.

Mr. Bones jotted down a note, "And these girls... how old were they?"

"Same age as me."

That was a relief! According to state law, if the girls were more than three years younger than Carlos, they would really have a problem on their hands. Then again, had that been the case, more than likely he wouldn't have been given the opportunity for probation.

"Did they send you pictures of themselves?"

"No, sir."

"Did they request pictures of you?"

"No, sir. I just..." Carlos paused and looked at his father. It was obvious he wanted to be anywhere but that office.

"You just, what?" Mr. Bones asked.

"I thought it would be funny."

Mr. Bones put his pen down. "Funny? How so?"

"I don't know. I guess it was a lack of judgment."

"Yeah, I'd say... Do you understand the seriousness of this offense, son?"

58

"Yes, sir."

Mr. Bones took a deep breath. The expression on the boy's face spoke nothing of remorse. Perhaps he was too young or too immature to grasp the significance of what had taken place. The probation officer turned his attention to the father for a moment, "Mr. Estrada, is this your son's first offense with something like this?"

"This is the furthest he has taken things… but he has acted out sexually for years."

"Has he ever touched anyone against their will?"

"No, sir. It's mostly just doing things to draw attention to himself."

Mr. Bones breathed a sigh of relief. It could be worse, "Is he seeing a counselor?"

"No, sir. We've tried that route but weren't very impressed with the results."

"I understand, but due to the nature of the crime at hand, I need you to take your son in for a psychological assessment. I want him in counseling for at least the next ninety days."

"Yes, sir… I can do that."

Mr. Bones picked his pen back up. It was time to add a higher level of awkwardness to the conversation. "Mr. Estrada… I hate to ask this, but has your son ever been sexually abused?"

Mr. Estrada shook his head, "No, not that I know of."

Mr. Bones tried to read the look in the boy's eyes, but he wasn't the easiest client to read. "Carlos? Has something gone on that your father isn't aware of?"

"No, sir."

"Would you tell me if someone had abused you?"

"Uh… probably not. But I don't know… I haven't been though."

"Okay. For now, I'm going to take your word for it."

Of all of the clients he had, Mr. Bones always struggled the most with ones assigned to him for sexual-related offenses. Far too often he saw young men like Carlos go on to become serious sexual offenders and end up with their names affixed to an offender registry for the rest of their lives.

Once the teen and his father left the office, Mr. Bones bowed his head at his desk. He whispered a prayer for God to deliver Carlos from the temptations that could quite possibly destroy his future.

It wasn't long before Rose brought Billy to his door, "Your frequent flyer's here."

"Thanks, Rose."

"No problem."

"Come on in, Billy."

Billy complied without uttering a word.

"Have a seat. I want to hear all about this stolen marker and the high you got from it."

10

Wearing an overstuffed backpack, Alden Wamboldt sat on the couch anxiously staring at the door.

"You might as well watch TV or something while you're waiting," his grandmother said.

Alden didn't take his eyes off the door. "I'm too excited!" he said.

"I remember when you hated spending time with that man."

Alden smiled, "Me too. But that was the old me."

A knock met their ears. "I'll get it!" Alden shouted before jumping out of his chair and sprinting to the door. Whipping it open, he grinned from ear to ear. "Do you want to come in or are we just going to head to your place?"

Mr. Bones chuckled. "Well, if you don't mind, I'd like to at least come in and say hi to your grandmother for a second. I'm sure she'd like to have the opportunity to meet Billy."

"Sure," Alden said, returning to his chair.

"Mrs. Wamboldt, this is—"

"Hi, Billy," she interrupted. "It's a pleasure to meet you."

"You as well, ma'am." Billy smiled at his probation officer as if the man owed him a cookie for being so mannerly.

"How has Alden been behaving himself?" Mr. Bones asked.

"Much better than he used to. I called the school this morning and Mr. Ponderosa said he's done fine other than that one hiccup the other day."

"Glad to hear that. Way to go, Alden!"

Alden grinned. Up until recently, receiving compliments had been somewhat of a rarity.

"I've got a lot to do this weekend," Mr. Bones said. "In addition to working with these guys, I've got to prepare my first sermon."

"Your first sermon?" Alden's smile broadened. "God did call you to preach?"

"He did indeed."

"When are you preaching?"

"Sunday evening."

"Grandma, I want to hear his first message!... Can I stay the whole weekend?"

Mrs. Wamboldt shook her head. "Alden, it's rude to overstay your welcome. Mr. Bones invited you to spend one night. Not two."

If there was one part of Alden's personality that hadn't changed, it was his stubbornness. Once his mind was set on something, it wasn't easily changed. "Can I stay an extra night, Mr. Bones? Please?"

"Alden," Mrs. Wamboldt snapped. "You don't invite yourself to stay somewhere; wait for an invitation." She looked at Mr. Bones, trying to gauge his thoughts on the matter.

"It's okay with me, Mrs. Wamboldt. He can stay until after church Sunday evening if that's okay with you."

"It's not a problem... What church do you go to? I might just come by myself and then Alden can return home with me afterward."

Mr. Bones smiled, "I would appreciate that, Mrs. Wamboldt. It's Clover Street Baptist Church, across from —"

"Oh, I know where that is! A friend of mine attends there. Do you know Shelby Benton?"

"I sure do. Fine Christian lady."

"That she is! I think I will come by. I haven't seen Shelby for quite some time. She'll be so surprised to see me."

"We would love to have you, ma'am."

"Fantastic... But I guess I better step out of your way so you boys can get your sleepover started."

Those were just the words Alden was waiting to hear. The teen jumped up and grabbed his backpack. "See you Sunday night," he said. "I love you, Grandma."

Mrs. Wamboldt grinned, "Mr. Bones, you are a tremendous blessing to my grandson. Thank you so much for everything you're doing!"

"You're welcome," Mr. Bones said before leading Billy and Alden outside. He and his protegees hadn't been in the car a whole minute before Billy looked at Alden and said, "You familiar with The Black Disciples, kid?"

Mr. Bones turned around, "Billy, we're not going to start this again!"

"Why? You don't want your little pet to know I'm in a gang? Don't want him to be afraid to sleep in the same house as me? Don't worry, Alden... I'm not gonna hurt you — not too bad anyway."

"Don't listen to him, Alden. Believe me, you're far more violent than he ever thought of being. If anybody ought to be afraid of going to sleep tonight, it ought to be Billy. He's not in a gang. It's just something he says to—"

"Shut up, Mr. Bones! Unless you want to see what I'm made of."

The probation officer hadn't started the car yet. He got out and jerked Billy's door open. The fourteen-year-old lunged out and got nose to nose with him.

Mr. Bones wasn't having it, "Alright, gang banga. You want some of this? Touch me, and we'll see how *street* you really are."

Billy balled his right hand into a fist and didn't blink an eye.

Mr. Bones challenged him, "What are you waiting for? Show us what you're made of, man."

Billy whirled around and pounded his fist against the roof of the car. "If you weren't my probation officer, I'd—"

"You wouldn't do a thing, and you know it! Get back in that car and get your seatbelt on!"

Billy complied but grumbled all the way back to the house. Once inside, he said, "Where's the kid gonna sleep? I ain't about to give up the futon!"

"You just did, Billy," Mr. Bones retorted.

"I just did what?"

"You just forfeited the futon. You don't come in my house and tell me what you are or aren't going to do!"

"So, what? You sayin' you gonna give this boy the couch and make me sleep on the floor 'cause he's white, and I'm black? You a racist, man. That's all there is to it!"

"You know what, Billy? I've had about enough of the whole race-card thing. I've taken you into my house, bought your food, and cooked your meals. I've tried to help you rebuild your relationship with your mother… and all I get from you is a bunch of grief. It's going to stop, and I mean right now."

"Sounds to me like somebody can't handle the truth!"

Alden had tried to keep his nose out of it, but he couldn't do it anymore. Billy was too much, and it sounded like Mr. Bones wasn't getting anywhere with him. He had to say something. Maybe, just maybe Billy would listen to one of his peers better than he would an adult. It was worth a shot anyway. "Billy, I used to be just like you. I hated Mr. Bones too. But he was trying to help me. I just—"

"Nobody asked you."

"That doesn't mean I can't speak my mind. I don't like the way you're treating Mr. Bones. He hasn't done anything to you."

"You ain't even been here. You don't know nothin'!"

Alden's eyes widened. "I'm trying to be polite here, man, but you're not making that very easy. So, stealing the words of our probation officer, I'm going to stop making bones about this. Back off and leave the man alone!"

"And if I don't?... Ain't like you and those noodle arms can do anything about it!"

Alden balled his fists, stretched out his fingers, and balled them again. "I will teach my anger it's not in control," he told himself. "I will not allow my anger to control me."

"Ah, ain't that cute?" Billy laughed. "You and Mr. B. tryin' to work together to make me think you're some kind of punk. Who in their right mind would be scared of you, ya little wimp?"

There went Alden's plan of controlling his anger! He gave Billy an uppercut, making the thug-wannabe fall backward and smack his head on the end table before hitting the floor. Overcome by uncontrollable rage, Alden took a glass off of the coffee table and had every intention of smashing it over Billy's head. Before he could, however, his probation officer grabbed him from behind and carefully, yet aggressively took him to the ground.

Billy lay on the floor stunned.

Alden tried to jerk his way free from his probation officer's grasp for a moment. Tears formed in his eyes. "Man!" he said. "I let my anger win another victory. I'm sorry, Mr. Bones. I didn't mean to."

Mr. Bones let him go, "Go plant yourself in the dining room; I'll deal with you in a minute."

"Yes, sir," Alden replied.

Mr. Bones walked over to Billy and knelt next to him, "You alright, bud?"

"Yeah. But I'll tell you one thing... That kid packs a powerful punch."

"He took it easy on you, Billy. That boy's known to use ball bats or whatever he can get his hands on. He's not the kind of kid for you to be messing with. And if I were you, I'd drop the whole gang nonsense. That's just going to make him see you as a bigger challenge."

"It better strike some fear into him."

"Yeah, that theory's not working out in your favor very well," Mr. Bones replied sarcastically. "You don't have to listen to me. Keep trying that approach... but don't blame me when you don't get the results you're looking for."

Billy didn't utter a word.

Mr. Bones, however, made sure his feelings on the matter were well known. "All week, I looked forward to tonight. I had hoped you and Alden would be able to get along. I thought perhaps the three of us could play a board game or watch a movie and pop some popcorn. But you guys have ruined it already. You go and act up at school, and now Alden loses his temper here at the house. I don't even know what to say."

What came out of Billy's mouth next took Mr. Bones completely off guard. "My uncle used to quote a Bible verse to me in times like this. Something about Jesus saying 'Father forgive them for they know not what they do.' You could always try to be like Jesus."

Mr. Bones couldn't help but smirk. "Pretty clever, my friend. But right now, I believe some discipline is in order."

11

By the time Sunday evening spun around, Philip was more worked up than a fly caught in the web of a black widow. After studying for hours after the boys went to bed, his most substantial fear was preaching too long. He couldn't believe Pastor Jahmal told him not to worry if his sermon was too short. He was certain that wouldn't be a problem.

Scanning the congregation, Philip recalled the first time he went off the diving board. That same feeling swept over him. He wanted to back away from the pulpit. To descend the steps and return to his seat. But if he was able to dive into that pool, he could plunge into the whole preaching thing as well.

"Help him, Lord!" a lady shouted.

"Yes, Jesus!" another voice chimed in.

Philip shakily opened his Bible and asked everyone to turn to the fifth chapter of Isaiah. With his heart rising into this throat, the preacher boy's voice cracked. Still, the sermon had to go on.

Philip preached with all of his might and was strengthened by a slew of "Amen's!" and "Praise the Lords!" Those sentiments of encouragement helped him make it through the entire sermon without making himself look like a fool. When he turned the service over to the pastor, he apologized for being so long-winded.

Pastor Jahmal chuckled, "Have you checked the clock, son?"

Directing his eyes to the rear of the sanctuary, Philip shook his head, "That can't be right."

Pastor Jahmal laughed again. "Happens to the best of us, brother. It's okay. A touch of stage fright brought you into a state of speed-talking. You'll get better. Just give it time and don't give up."

Philp blinked his eyes a few times and stared at the clock again, "There's no way I preached that entire sermon in five minutes!"

"You did, brother. But don't sweat it. For a first sermon, that was fantastic."

Philip felt his face turning red. He was more humiliated than he had ever been in his life.

As he took his seat, Alden patted him on the back, "Way to go, Mr. Bones! You were great!"

Somehow, that didn't make Philip feel any better. He appreciated Alden's attempt to comfort him, but it only added to his level of embarrassment.

Billy called Alden a suck-up before taunting his probation officer, "Five minutes, man? That's all you got? And you call yourself a preacher?"

Mr. Bones shook his head and put a finger to his lips. The pastor was speaking, and their commotion was disturbing everyone around them. As the boys closed their traps, the pastor was in the middle of saying, "I don't want to add or take away from the brother's message this evening. I believe what we just heard was a message straight from the Lord! Can I get a witness?"

After a few loud "Amen's," the pastor asked for testimonies. Mrs. Wamboldt stood up in the back. "I want to thank the good Lord for that young man who just spoke. He has been mentoring my grandson, and he's had a huge impact on him. I appreciate God bringing him into our lives. Thank you, Philip!"

Billy mumbled, "Whatever."

Mr. Bones ignored the petty jab but Alden wasn't about to let it go. Elbowing him in the ribs, he ordered Billy to shut up.

"Oh, no you didn't!" Billy snapped.

Alden grinned mischievously, "Oh, yes I did and that was the only warning you're going to get. Shut up and I mean it!"

"Boys, cut it out!... Both of you," Mr. Bones said quietly.

"Yes, sir," Alden replied.

Billy simply turned his head the other way.

As soon as the service was over, Mr. Bones released Alden into his grandmother's care. As they finished their goodbyes, an elderly couple stopped and invited Philip to their place for dinner. "I appreciate the offer," he told them as he turned to look at Billy, "but I have a few matters I need to deal with this evening."

"Hmph," Billy said.

"You folks enjoy the rest of your week," Philip told them. "Come on, Billy, we need to get to the house."

The trip home was fairly quiet but once they got inside, all of that changed. Mr. Bones was not impressed with some of the behaviors he had seen over the weekend — especially not with Billy's attitude at church. "I don't know how much more of this I can take. Why are you so on edge all of the time?"

"You think *I'm* moody? You ever listen to yourself?"

"This is about you, not me!" Mr. Bones retorted.

"Why? Because you say that's what it's about? Opinions are like toilet paper, you know? Everybody has some. If you can share yours, you better expect to hear mine!"

"This isn't about opinions, Billy; it's about facts. There's no need for rudeness, especially not in the Lord's house."

"Tell me about it."

Mr. Bones was going to tell him about it alright. Somebody sure needed to! "I'm talking about you, Billy. The way you insulted me about my sermon. The dirty looks you were giving Alden. The way you responded to his grandmother's testimony. Your attitude when I told those folks I couldn't come over for dinner. That kind of behavior is completely unacceptable."

"Man, why you be talkin' to me like I'm your son or somethin'? Did you forget you're just my probation officer? You ain't my daddy!"

"Be thankful for that," Mr. Bones replied. "I may not be your father, but I am the man who is putting a roof over your head and food in your stomach. I am the adult who is keeping you off of the streets and the one who is going to make you follow my rules whether you want to or not."

"I ain't broke no rules, Mr. Bones. Ain't smoked no weed, ain't drank no beer, ain't used no foul language, been in bed on time every night, been coming by your office every day after school."

Mr. Bones shook his head in exasperation. After giving himself a moment to collect his thoughts, he said, "Billy, I appreciate you following the rules I laid out for you when you first came here. But it's not too difficult to pick up on some of my other expectations. You're not living up to your potential. Kindness goes a long way."

"So now there's a rule I have to follow about being kind? Come on, Mr. Bones! This is getting out of hand."

The fourteen-year-old was right about that. Things were getting out of hand, but it wasn't on account of his probation officer. It was time for Mr. Bones to step up his game. "Billy, I'm starting to pick up on something with you."

"What's that?"

"You're not the type of young man who is going to learn from being lectured. Everything seeps into one ear and gushes out the other."

Billy raised his voice, "Oh, so now you gonna do what you little pet suggested last night?"

"Alden is not my pet, and the answer to your question is a resounding no. The island method isn't for everybody... With you, we're going to try something different."

"Like what?"

"Like... for starters, you're going to begin receiving consequences that better match the offense."

"And how is that any different than normal?"

"Let me show you. So, tonight in church you criticized the length of my sermon. Now you have three days to prepare one of your own. After church Wednesday evening you're going to preach to me for thirty minutes."

Billy sported a fake smile, "No problem... Hope you don't mind hearing a message on hypocrisy!"

Mr. Bones should have seen that one coming. It was a good thing he was a fast thinker. "Actually, you don't get to choose the topic. Since it's discipline, that's my call. Your lesson will be on submission to authority."

"And how you expect me to go about finding verses on that?"

"You can use the concordance in the back of your Bible, or I can help you."

"I ain't need no help from you, Mr. Bones."

"Good, Billy. I'll be looking forward to hearing your sermon."

12

It was 4:00 in the afternoon; with Billy not showing up after school, Philip was becoming uneasy. He headed down the hall to check the restrooms and parking lot. After giving the building a thorough search, Philip realized the teenager's honeymoon period had probably worn off. Upset that his probation officer had been cracking down on him, more than likely Billy didn't report to the office out of defiance — or because he had gotten himself into legal trouble somewhere along the way.

Philip went back to his office. Thankfully, no clients had shown up. Closing his door, he called Tamara and got her voicemail, "Tamara, hi… it's Philip Bones, Billy's probation officer. He didn't report to me after school today, and I'm concerned about his welfare. If you've seen him by any chance, please give me a call and let me know. Okay?... If I don't hear from him soon, I'm going to clock out and see if I can hunt him down. Thanks."

Rose tapped on the door.

"Is Billy out there?" Philip asked.

"Afraid not… but Dennis is here for his check-in."

"Is he the last one on the docket today?"

"Yes, sir."

"Send him back... And, Rose, if Billy doesn't show up by the time I'm through with this meeting, I'm going to have to go look for him."

Rose sighed, "Don't you think you're missing a lot of work lately, Philip?"

Philip didn't want to hear it. He didn't have to answer to his secretary. "Send Dennis in," he said without acknowledging her question.

Rose took the hint. "Yes, sir. On the double."

Dennis was one of those clients Philip always tried to rush out of his office. It wasn't because the extremely overweight sixteen-year-old wasn't friendly. It was because — there came the putrid odor of body funk. Dennis strolled in and started to close the door. "It's okay. Leave it as it is, please," Philip said while spinning his chair around and sliding the window open.

"Wassup, Mr. Philly?"

The probation officer's eyes almost rolled involuntarily, but he managed to get them under control. "Why do you always call me that?... You know my name is Mr. Bones."

Dennis smiled, "But Mr. Philly fits you a lot better."

Mr. Bones tried to look him in the eye, but the giant white-headed zit on the top of his nose was downright repulsive. Not to mention the kid's hair looked like a tangled, greasy mess as usual. Looking down at his desk, Mr. Bones said, "Alright, Dennis... you know I have a busy schedule. Let's get down to business, shall we?"

"Might as well," Dennis replied.

"Did you go to school today?"

"Yep."

Short answers like that one always aroused suspicion. "Did you stay all day?"

Dennis yawned a loud, somewhat audible, "Yeah."

"Did you skip any classes?"

"Today?... No... Well, not that I remember anyway."

What a lovely answer! Mr. Bones detested that kind of response. He knew what the kid was doing — making it so if he was caught in a lie, he could later have a loophole. It wasn't worth fighting about it. He just needed to get the appointment done and over with, so he could spray some air freshener and begin his hunt for a missing client. "How about yesterday? Did you skip any classes yesterday?"

Dennis looked at the ceiling for a moment before mumbling, "Just Algebra."

"Dennis, you could have your probation revoked for that. You can't pick and choose which classes to attend."

"I know. You've told me."

"So, you don't think I'll do it? Is that it?"

"Mr, Philly, you know the judge won't take me off of probation." He chuckled, "The state couldn't afford to feed me."

The disrespect Dennis had for himself was nearly infuriating. Mr. Bones shook his head, "You shouldn't put yourself down like that."

"It's true!... Do you have any idea how much I eat every day?"

"Not a clue."

"I could out-eat a pregnant elephant — even if she was carrying triplets."

"Why don't you do something about your weight then?"

Dennis laughed. "Maybe I like being different; ever think of that?"

"Oh, please," Mr. Bones muttered. "Okay, look. I'm going to put a note in your file; if you skip any more classes this semester, I'm going to petition the judge to revoke your right to probation. Got me?"

"I hear ya, Mr. Philly."

"I plan to check in with your guidance counselor on a weekly basis. Don't let me get a bad report."

"No worries. If I think she might say something bad about me, I'll slit her throat." Dennis chuckled again.

"Please don't laugh about things like that," Mr. Bones told him.

"You don't have a good sense of humor, do you, Mr. Philly?"

If that kid said Mr. Philly one more time, the probation officer feared he might throw him through the wall. For the boy's safety, he had to get Dennis out of the building as soon as possible. "Okay... we need to wrap this up," he said. "Everything else going okay?"

"Yeah. I guess so."

"Good. In that case, you can see yourself out. I'll be looking forward to meeting with you next month."

"Cool beans."

Philip was thrilled to death to see the annoying teenager leave his office while he was still in one piece. After giving him a minute, he walked back out to his reception's desk. "Billy still hasn't shown up?"

"No, sir... Sorry."

"That's what I was afraid of... I'm heading out."

Rose was clearly not happy with Philip's decision, but she kept her thoughts to herself.

Philip drove the route he thought Billy would have taken from his school to the courthouse. There were no signs of him. Parking at the school, he approached the door. It was locked:

there was no indication that a ball game or extracurricular event was being held.

Dialing Tamara's number again, Philip was discouraged by still not receiving an answer. He wasn't about to leave a second voicemail. Hopping back in his car, the probation officer drove up and down streets and alleys for a couple of hours, occasionally getting out and asking people if they had seen the boy. Short on leads, Philip drove to Tamara's place and knocked on the door. To his surprise, Billy answered, "What you want, Bones?"

The probation officer was livid, "I have been searching for you for hours! What are you doing here? Where's your mother?"

"Don't you be gettin' an attitude with my son," Tamara shouted in the background. "Billy, you get in here and let me take care of this man!"

Mr. Bones was shocked. He thought maybe the boy had gone there on his own to hide out for a while — the last thing he had expected was to find Tamara home.

Billy smirked and walked back inside.

Tamara stomped to the door and cocked her head, "You have some nerve coming here, Mr. Bones!" she screamed.

Mr. Bones had no idea what she was upset about. "Did I do something wrong?"

"You are somethin' else! Demanding my baby preach a sermon when the good Lord ain't called him to be no preacher! What kind of blaspheme is that?"

"I'm trying to teach your son a lesson about respecting others."

Tamara put one hand on her hip. "You talk me into lettin' my son move in with you, and then you pull somethin' like this?"

Mr. Bones was as confused as all get out as Tamara continued bawling him out, "I may not be a church-goer, but I have enough fear of the Lord to know better than to mess with Him. It ain't right to use God to be gettin' back at somebody!"

"I'm not using God to do anything," Mr. Bones replied.

"You might be able to convince yourself of that, Mr. Bones, but I, for one, ain't buyin' it! You know what? You get off of my property! You weren't invited here!"

"Mrs. Andrews, are you—"

"Leave now, Mr. Bones, or I'm going to call the police and report you for trespassing!"

It was bad enough when clients seemed to have multiple personalities, but when their parents did, it made mentoring nearly impossible.

13

After mowing the lawn, Billy meandered inside to find a note:

> Went out with some girlfriends.
> Be back late tonight,
>
> Momma

Fine, Billy told himself. *If you're going out, so am I!* The fourteen-year-old barged into his mother's room and swiped the twenty-dollar bill laying on her dresser. It wasn't much, but it would have to do.

Billy knew none of the convenience stores in the area would sell him any of the good stuff — that's where having a twenty-one-year-old friend came in handy. Billy walked down the block to Tyrone's place. "Hey man, I'm looking for a drinking buddy — you game?"

"I'd love to, Billy but this boy is b-r-o-k-e."

"I got twenty bucks here, man."

"Sweet..." Tyrone slipped his sandals on. "Hang here, and I'll go across the street and get us some beers."

While his friend was away, Billy made himself right at home. Pilfering through the fridge, he helped himself to a plate of leftover lasagna, knowing Tyrone wouldn't mind. Knowing Tyrone, if Billy didn't eat it, it would end up growing mold and being tossed in the garbage anyway.

Billy was still stuffing his face when Tyrone returned with their buddy, Mark. The guys cranked up some music and got their party going. Within an hour, they were completely plastered.

With the alcohol making him irritable, Billy turned on Tyrone, "Where's that watch I sold you?"

"What watch?"

"The one I told you I got from my daddy... I want it back, Ty."

"You want it back? Are you crazy?"

"I wasn't thinking when I sold it to you, man. It has sentimental value."

"It's not for sale."

"Come on, man. This is important to me."

"So?"

Billy stood and staggered toward him, "You have no idea how much trouble I got in for selling that thing. I need it."

"How badly?"

"I'd give anything man. My wallet, my shoes, my firstborn child... anything!"

"Really?..." Tyrone laughed. "How's $2,000 sound to you?"

Billy raised his voice, "$2,000?... It ain't worth but $800."

Tyrone chuckled again, "Thanks for the information, man. I got myself quite the bargain then, didn't I?"

"Please, Tyrone... I thought we were friends."

"We are, Billy. But I'm not quite as tight with you as I am with that pile of greenbacks. You hear me?"

Mark staggered over, "Tyrone, don't be like that. It belonged to his dad. The man died, remember?"

"Yeah. So?"

"Give it to him, man."

"And what you gonna do about it if I don't?"

Mark chest-bumped Tyrone, "Give it to the boy!"

Tyrone shoved him backward, leaving Billy little choice but to step between the two, "Stop guys. It ain't worth this."

Mark knocked Billy out of his way and tackled Tyrone to the ground. He threw a couple of punches, ignoring Billy's pleas for him to stop. Billy grabbed Mark from the back and jerked him off of Tyrone. It was the right thing to do — but it backfired. Tyrone swung at Mark but in his drunken state, hit the wrong person. Blood oozed from Billy's lip.

"See what you did, now?" Mark shouted. "You just assaulted a minor!" With that, he gave Tyrone a second beating.

Billy rushed out of the house, struggling to hold his pants up as he went. He wanted no part of whatever went down in there.

When he got back to the house, he was shocked to find his mother pulling into the driveway. "You're early, Momma."

"And you've been fighting!" she scolded.

"I had a good reason, Momma."

"Ain't never no good reason for fighting. Let's get you inside so I can have a look at that lip."

"I'm fine, Momma. It ain't no big deal."

"I'll make that decision." Tamara grabbed his ear, "Inside... march!"

Instead of telling his mother what really took place, Billy said, "I took a walk, and while I's out, I ran into that crook that swindled me outta Daddy's pocket watch. I told him you wanted to buy it back and the buster laughed in my face. I tried to reason with him, Momma. I told him all about how Daddy died and about how it belonged to his daddy before him. But the dude didn't care 'bout nothin' but his money."

"So, you hit him?"

"Well... yeah! What'd you expect me to do, Momma? Just let him hold onto Daddy's watch?"

His mother half-smiled, "So, you got it back from him?"

"I tried to, Momma."

"You tried to? You found the guy that has that watch, and you didn't get it from him?"

"Momma, I tried!"

"Not hard enough! Go to your room. I can't even stand the sight of you!"

"But, Momma—"

"Now, Billy!"

Billy shook his head while stomping to his room. Sometimes he couldn't stand living in that house. He'd rather sleep under a bridge than put up with her attitude.

For half an hour or so, he laid there sulking. He would have continued longer had his mom not barged into the room and threw the phone at him. "Talk to the man," she snapped.

"Who is it?"

"Just pick up the phone and talk to him. You'll find out."

"Fine," Billy grumbled, pulling the phone up to his ear. "Who this be?"

"Billy, it's Mr. Bones... I understand you got yourself into a boxing match."

How did his probation officer find out about it so quickly? It didn't matter. What was done was done. "So... what of it?"

"You violated your probation," Mr. Bones said.

"Lock me up then!... See if I care!"

"It might just come to that, Billy. Your mother called me because she's concerned about you."

Billy glared at his mom. That explained how Mr. Bones found out about it — she had gone and snitched on him! "Momma ain't concerned about nobody but herself," Billy said hatefully.

"Your mother loves you, Billy. She feels like this wouldn't have happened had she made you go through with preaching that sermon. It's important for you to learn to accept responsibility for your actions. That's why she called me."

Billy smirked, "She just telling you what you want to hear, Mr. Bones. That's Momma for you — the queen manipulator herself. She ain't sorry. She just want me outta her hair."

"I don't believe that, Billy... Regardless though, I want to know your thoughts. Do you want to come back to my place for a while?"

That was a stupid question if Billy ever heard one. "Nah, man. You got too many rules."

"So, you'd rather stay where you are?"

"No... I'd rather be behind bars. Just tell that old judge I ain't be deserving no probation. Tell him I belong in juvie, man."

Mr. Bones sighed, "Let me talk to your mother, please."

"Gladly."

Billy listened as his mother said, "So, you gonna come pick him up or shall I bring him to you?... What?... You're blaming me?... What gives you the right?... I did not take away your authority with my son!... No, I did not!... So, you won't let him stay with you?... I thought you cared about teenagers... Oh yeah, it's only the white ones you concern yourself with — what was I thinking?... Fine, fine, okay... I can come by tomorrow morning... will 11:30 work?... Yeah, yeah. See you then."

Not hearing the other side of the conversation, Billy felt himself tensing up. "What was that all about?" he asked as his mother hung up the phone.

"I don't rightly know. Your probation officer wants me to stop by his office in the morning so we can talk."

Billy smiled innocently, "So, I get to miss school?"

"No, Billy. He wants to meet with me. He specifically said not to bring you along."

Billy raised his voice. "What?... He can't do that! You ain't on probation; I am. Ain't no reason for you and him to be talkin' when I ain't around!"

"Yes, he can do that, Billy. I'll let you know what it's about when you get home from school tomorrow. Okay?"

"Yeah, whatever."

14

A meeting with Tamara Andrews was certain to be about as pleasant of an experience as hugging a porcupine, but it was the only way. If Mr. Bones couldn't reach her, Billy would continue spiraling further and further out of control.

"So, what's the deal, Mr. Bones? I'm assuming you have a new game plan for my son?"

"I do have something in mind. I believe I know how to get his attention, but it's going to require diligent teamwork."

"I ain't got no problem with that. What you want me to do?"

Mr. Bones leaned forward in his chair, "Mrs. Andrews—"

"Please call me Tamara."

"Sorry about that..." Mr. Bones said. "Tamara, Billy is the type of young man who needs to have his will broken through harsh penalties. He likes to play one adult against another. I would love to continue working with your son outside of my normal work hours. However, it's not going to do the boy any good if you and I cannot stay on the same page."

Tamara pursed her lips, "I don't see why that should be a problem."

That was what Mr. Bones was afraid of. The woman didn't get it. She truly didn't understand how her poor decisions were causing her son to fail in life. How could he get her to understand without starting a war that would inevitably end with Billy's defeat?

Mr. Bones would have to choose his words carefully. "Ma'am, you love that child; I can see that," he began. "But sometimes love can't be gentle; nor can it be overly protective. Billy requires firm, consistent consequences — from both of us. And he can never, under any circumstances, get the upper hand by turning us against one another."

"So, you and I are always right, and Billy is always wrong?... Is that what you're saying?"

The sarcasm in her voice was unmistakable. If Mr. Bones weren't careful, the lady he was trying to form an alliance with would soon become his enemy. "Not exactly... but yeah, I guess... kind of."

"Listen, Mr. Bones. I wasn't born last night — If I agree to never get upset with you no matter what my son tells me, I would be giving you the liberty to abuse him any way you choose."

Mr. Bones sighed, "This isn't going to work, Tamara. I might as well petition the judge to have his probation revoked."

"What?" Tamara snapped. "Why won't it work?"

"Because you are not willing to allow anyone to reach your son."

"So, you're back to this thing about blaming me for all of my son's problems?"

Mr. Bones couldn't tell her to wear the shoe if it fit, even though the words were teetering on the tip of his tongue. Somehow he had to get her to take the blinders off. "Not entirely," he said. "Billy is old enough to make decisions for himself. He can choose to do right, or he can choose to do wrong... However, you are making it easier for him to be disobedient. You have good intentions but shielding your son from discipline is the worst decision you can make."

Tamara started fiddling with one of her earrings.

"Do you understand what I'm saying?" Mr. Bones asked her.

"Oh, I understand alright! You're just like everybody else. Gonna tell me the apple don't fall very far from the tree. Not like I ain't never heard that one before."

Mr. Bones leaned back in his chair. "Tamara, the choice is yours. You can allow me to work with your son or you can continue raising him the way you have been without my assistance. But... ask yourself this — how has that been working out for you? The young man is stealing from people, he never takes responsibility for anything he does wrong, he's manipulative... Do you truly believe any of that will improve if you keep training him the same way you have been?"

Tamara shook her head.

"Thank you for being honest... Neither do I."

"What do you suggest, Mr. Bones?"

Mr. Bones was hoping she would ask that. He had given the situation a great deal of thought and prayer. "I would like to try an approach I refer to as the 'Get What's Coming To You' method."

Tamara snickered, "What's that mean?"

Things were turning around. Tamara was beginning to listen, and it appeared, at least for the time being, that the two would be able to form an alliance after all. "Well, for beginners," the probation officer said, "like I told Billy at my place, he needs to start receiving consequences that closely match his behaviors."

"Like the sermon?"

"Exactly! He needs to study for a sermon so he can see how much work goes into one. He then needs to present it to the best of his ability — it was just going to be in my presence, but now that he manipulated you to get out of his consequence, he needs to present it to both of us."

"I'm down with that plan," Tamara said.

"And after he does, no matter how good it sounds, neither one of us can compliment him. Instead, we're going to critique the fire out of his sermon."

"Even if he does a fantastic job?"

"Oh, yeah! He needs to get what's coming to him."

"Okay," Tamara smiled. "What else you got?"

Mr. Bones appreciated her enthusiasm. He wasn't sure what changed, but her entire attitude was different. He hoped his next idea wouldn't do away with the progress he had made. "Tamara, do you feel you're a strong disciplinarian?"

Tamara took a deep breath. "To be honest, no... But I don't know how to change that."

"I can help you in that area... Going forward, when Billy acts up, I want you to send him to his room like you did the other night. After his door's closed, step outside so Billy can't hear you and secretly give me a call. We will figure out his consequences together. It's important that you don't allow Billy to figure out you're calling. That will undermine your authority with him."

"Wait a minute!" Tamara said, with her eyes growing wide. "Are you saying Billy's going to be staying with me? I thought he was going to return to your place for a while?"

The truth be known — Mr. Bones would have loved that. But he couldn't. Not after what happened the first time. It would only be setting the kid up for failure. "That wouldn't work," Mr. Bones told her. "Billy has already seen that he could play that to his advantage. We have to do things differently now."

Tamara shook her head. "I know what you're saying, Mr. Bones. You're afraid I'll interfere again."

"Tamara, I'm not going to make any bones about this. Over the years, I've engaged in many battles with families of struggling teenagers. I will do my best to help you and your son. At the same time, when one firecracker blows up in my face, I'm not going to set another one on my kitchen table. Does that make sense?"

Tamara snickered. "I get you, Mr. Bones. But I'm not going to sneak and take Billy back to the house again. If he's staying with you, he's staying with you. It's that cut and dry."

"Not this time, Tamara. He has already gone from your house to mine and then returned to your house again. Passing him back and forth isn't going to teach him a thing. He needs to stay in one place and follow the rules that are set for him."

Tamara didn't seem too sure. "And what if this doesn't work?"

"We'll give it six weeks. If his behavior doesn't improve, we'll try a different approach."

"Okay, so he stays with me; when he misbehaves, you help me decide on age-appropriate discipline. Is that all?"

Mr. Bones smirked, "That's only the beginning of the plan. The other part may sound slightly dirty, and it will undoubtedly make your son hostile — toward both of us when he finds out we're in it together. But once he cools down, I believe it will teach him a lesson he will never forget. Here's the plan..."

15

It was 6:00 am on Saturday morning when Mr. Bones lightly tapped on the door to the Andrews' place, hoping Tamara was going to stick to their plan. Within seconds, she quietly opened the door, "Come on in," she whispered. "He's not going to be very happy about this."

"I don't expect him to be," Mr. Bones replied. "He's going to get what's coming to him."

"That he is," Tamara snickered. "Here's the agreement you wanted me to sign."

"Awesome," Mr. Bones said, looking it over. "You won't regret this. Where's his room? I'll give him a surprise wake-up call."

Tamara smirked, "Better you than me. Down the hall, second door on the right."

Philip was slightly nervous about waking the teen up so early, especially when Billy had no idea he was coming over. Swallowing his fear, he tried the knob — it was unlocked.

Inside, he found Billy laying on his side, loudly chewing the air. *Must be eating some wind-pudding,* Philip told himself. Tiptoeing next to the bed, the probation officer put his hands just above Billy's head and clapped them five times.

Billy jumped, "Whoa, whoa, whoa, whoa!... What are you doing here, Mr. Bones? The sun ain't even up yet!"

"Time to rise and shine," Mr. Bones said.

"What?... It's Saturday, man!" Billy tugged the blankets over his head. "I ain't getting up. Not 'til at least noon."

Mr. Bones jerked the covers off of him, "Wrong! You're getting an early start today."

Billy partially opened his eyes, "What's this all about, Mr. B.?"

Mr. Bones grabbed the teen's arm and pulled him into a seated position, "Get up and get dressed. We'll talk about it in the living room."

"Momma know you're here?"

Mr. Bones laughed. He understood Billy's hesitance. He couldn't even imagine how he would have felt if the roles had been reversed. "She does. She'll be waiting in the living room as well... By the way, bring your Bible with you when you come out."

"This is crazy," Billy complained. "Give me a couple of minutes, and I'll be out."

"Three minutes," Mr. Bones said.

"Three minutes 'til what?"

"Til I come back in here and drag you down that hall. Don't go back to sleep. I'm going out to talk with your mom."

Mr. Bones looked at his watch for effect before exiting the room.

Tamara was taking a seat in the living room when Mr. Bones came in. "Just finished whipping up some buttermilk pancakes and boiled eggs," she said.

"Wonderful. That'll help. Don't forget... no matter how good he does, we cannot compliment him under any circumstances."

"I know. I've been practicing in front of my mirror. I'm ready."

In just under three minutes, Billy joined them in the living room. "Do I smell breakfast already?"

"You do," Tamara said.

"Why we be in the living room then? Ain't the food gonna get cold?"

"Well," Mr. Bones said. "You were supposed to preach a sermon for me Wednesday evening. Remember?"

"Yeah. But I wasn't at your crib. I was here with my momma."

"That you were. But you were given a consequence, and you're expected to accept it."

"What?"

"Did you study for the sermon?"

"A little... but I didn't think I'd have to do it."

"Well, you do," Tamara interjected.

"And if I don't?"

"You won't eat," she snapped.

"Momma, you ain't gonna just throw that food away!"

"No, Billy, I won't. Your probation officer and I will eat until we're full and you can have what's left — after you've preached your sermon. Doesn't matter to me if it's in the next little bit or if you wait until after lunch or dinner. But you get it done within the next forty-five minutes, and we'll warm that breakfast back up for you. Any later than that, and you'll eat it cold."

"Momma! This ain't like you. Has Mr. B. brainwashed you or something?"

"It's the way things are going to be, Billy. If you've got a sermon ready, it's time to preach it."

"In front of both of you?"

"Yes, sir," Mr. Bones interjected.

"Alright. Fine. I got this. Ya'll gonna follow along in your Bibles?"

"We sure are," Tamara said. "Make us proud, son."

The probation officer gave her a dirty look. She had better not compliment or encourage him. If she didn't stick to their plan, it would ruin everything!

"Okay, good then," Billy said, flipping his Bible open. "I want us to have a look at Hebrews chapter thirteen, verse seventeen."

Mr. Bones and Tamara opened their Bibles while Billy waited patiently. When he saw they were there, he said, "The Good Book say to 'Obey them that have the rule over you, and submit yourselves: for they watch for your souls, as they that must give account, that they may do it with joy, and not with grief: for that is unprofitable for you.' Now, peoples, I want you to understand what this verse be sayin'. We got to be obeyin' those higher powers. You know what I'm sayin'? I mean... can I get a witness?"

Mr. Bones and Tamara looked at each other; neither gave Billy the "amen" he was expecting.

Looking confused, Billy continued, "When a man gets a job, for example, his boss tells him what hours to work. If that man submits to them that have the rule over him, he'll work when he's supposed to. Won't be leavin' early. Won't be skipping out. Won't be worryin' 'bout no other matters. Certainly won't be lyin' or being dishonest about it. He gonna submit to that boss. Ain't that right, Mr. Bones?"

94

Mr. Bones reluctantly nodded, seeing exactly how Billy planned on preaching his sermon.

"I'll tell ya what else it means!..." Billy preached for fourteen minutes, stomping all over both his probation officer's and his mother's shoes, pointing out each and every weakness he felt either one of them had.

At the end, he asked, "How was that?"

"I've heard better," Mr. Bones replied. "Sounded like you were preaching from the flesh. You didn't read the scriptures to obtain any kind of understanding at all. You used them maliciously; that's not the way the Bible's intended to be used."

"Whatever, man! That's how you preached! I don't wanna hear that... What'd you think, Momma?"

"I thought...," she hesitated for a moment and looked at Mr. Bones. "I thought you did..." she paused again.

"What'd you think, Momma?"

Mr. Bones glared at her, hoping to remind her of their negativity pact.

"I thought you did a good job reading, but that's the best I can say about it, Billy. My grandma took me to her church one time when they had a youth-led service. They had a third-grade little boy in there who volunteered to preach. Now, let me tell you something — that little man could preach."

"And you're saying I couldn't?"

"Not like that little guy."

"You sayin' a third-grader could out-preach me?"

Tamara laughed. "Honey, you should have heard the people in that church testifying afterward. Their testimonies were more powerful than your sermon. How much time do you spend studying for that thing? Two minutes? You gotta put your all into things, Billy. You can't take the easy way out."

Billy's lip jutted out as he hung his head and started for his room.

"Where are you going, boy?" Mr. Bones asked.

"Where's it look like?"

"It looks like you're going back to bed. Ain't happening, son."

Billy turned around. "I done told you, Mr. Bones. I ain't your son. But why can't I go to bed? I done did what you told me to."

"Now it's time for breakfast."

"Ain't hungry."

Mr. Bones stood, "I didn't ask if you were hungry. Your mother got up early and made this breakfast for you. Now, you're going to eat it. Let's head to the kitchen."

Billy stared at him for a moment without speaking.

Tamara snapped her fingers, "You heard the man. Scoot those feet into that kitchen!"

With a constipated expression on his face, Billy complied. He ate his breakfast in silence as Mr. Bones and Tamara talked and laughed as if they had been life-long friends.

As soon as they finished eating, Tamara instructed Billy to load the dishwasher.

"I ain't 'bout to do no such thing. That's women's work."

"Billy," Mr. Bones said sternly.

"What is this? You two teamin' up against me?"

"Load the dishwasher, Billy," Mr. Bones ordered. "And for backtalking, once you get it loaded, I want you to sweep and mop the floor."

"You can't be serious!"

"Do you want to clean the restroom next?"

Billy put on his pouty face, "I'll clean the kitchen... Just stay outta my way!"

Mr. Bones and Tamara sat at the table and continued to enjoy their conversation while watching the frustrated teen complete his chores.

"May I please go back to bed now?" he asked upon finishing.

"No way," Mr. Bones told him. "We have work to do."

"What you talkin' about? I just worked myself near to death while the two of you's been sitting over there chillin'."

Tamara spoke up, "Mr. Bones and I have come to an agreement, Billy."

"I ain't movin' back into that man's house."

"You will do whatever you're told to do," she barked.

"Ah, come on, Momma! I ain't like that man. I ain't like his rules. Ain't like his personality. Ain't like his house. Don't make me go there. Please, Momma!"

Tamara smiled, "Stop being rude, Billy... For now, your living arrangements will stay the same. But that can change at any time. If your probation officer and I feel it's in your best interests for you to live elsewhere, you will have no say so in the matter."

"But Momma—"

"But Momma nothing," Tamara snapped. "It's high time you be learnin' the value of hard work."

"I know how to work!"

"Maybe so," Mr. Bones interjected, "but you see nothing wrong with taking money and items other people have worked for."

Billy crossed his arms, "And?"

"We believe you won't be so quick to steal from others once you learn how difficult a day's work can be."

"Yeah, we'll see about that... Good night, ya'll."

"Wrong again, bud," Mr. Bones said. "You and I are heading out for a job."

"I ain't do no more work unless I gettin' paid for it."

Mr. Bones knew that was coming. Billy was falling right into the plan without even knowing it. "Oh, you'll be earning money alright," he said.

"How much?"

"Fifty bucks."

Billy smiled. "Now that's what I be talkin' 'bout. What we be waitin' around here for?"

Mr. Bones appreciated the boy's enthusiasm, but he didn't want him to get too excited. "We're going to go in just a minute but first let me explain how this is going to work. For the next six Saturdays, I'm going to swing by here and pick you up at 6:00 am. I'll be taking you out to complete various work assignments. They will all be paid tasks. But—"

"I know what that word 'but' means, Mr. Bones. What's the catch?"

"You won't get the money until the end of the six weeks. I'm going to hold onto it until you've completed every task you've been assigned."

"What?... Why?... It's my money!"

"When you get a job, you don't get paid as soon as the day's over. Usually, a guy has to work five days a week for two weeks in a row before he gets his first check. That's ten days, Billy. I'm trying to teach you how the real world operates. You will work six entire days before you see the money. Got me?"

"I don't like it, but I'm guessing I ain't got a choice in the matter."

"And that would be an accurate assessment," Mr. Bones replied.

Billy dropped the attitude. "What kind of work we gonna be doing?"

"First of all, you're going to be doing the work; I'm supervising. The jobs will be different every week. No matter what kind of work people do, it takes a lot out of them, and I want you to learn that first hand. When people earn their money, they expect to keep what they earn."

"Okay... so what are we doing today?"

"Get in the car, and you'll find out."

"Why can't you just tell me?"

Tamara jumped into the conversation, "Did you not hear your probation officer? Enough with that lip, Billy! Get in the car, and I'll see you later!"

16

That house was so full of poop that Billy thought he was going to lose his pancakes.

"So, what? Am I supposed to gather eggs or somethin'?"

Mr. Bones chuckled. "Do you really think that would be worth fifty dollars? Nice try, bud."

Billy shook his head, "I ain't picking up no bird manure. I hope that ain't what you be thinkin'."

Mr. Bones nodded, "Cleaning up the chicken houses are going to be the first part of your assignment."

As far as Billy was concerned, his probation officer had lost his mind. He hadn't played with animal feces since his tenth birthday, and he had no intentions of doing it at fourteen. "Whoa, whoa, whoa, whoa! Did you say hous*es* as in more than one?"

"Yes, sir," Mr. Bones said confidently. "Millie has six of them."

"Ah, man. Tell me they ain't all as big as this one."

Mr. Bones laughed. "They're all different sizes, man. But I believe this is the smallest one."

"No way! Huh-uh! I ain't doing this, Mr. B. I ain't no chicken farmer!"

Chuckling, his probation officer said, "Oh, you're going to do it. It won't kill you. Here, let me show you how." Picking up the hoe, he began scraping dried manure off of the floor. "See, nothing to it. Once you get it loose, take the shovel and toss it in the wheelbarrow."

The man described poop-handling as if it was a normal, everyday activity. What could possibly be gross about picking up some nasty critter's waste products? Billy had never even changed a wet baby diaper, let alone picked up poop that couldn't even be wrapped in anything. Shaking his head, Billy whined, "Mr. B., please don't make me do this."

"Stop with the Mr. B."

"Fine, Mr. Bones. Please. I'll do anything else. This ain't me." Billy didn't know why he even tried. His probation officer wasn't going to give him an inch. But there was always that shimmer of hope.

"It's okay," Mr. Bones replied. "You're going to do this work to the best of your ability. I'll be hanging out outside. Let me know if you encounter any—"

Billy jumped back at the sight of a plump, brown hen strutting up the ramp and coming through a small door opposite where they were standing. "Ah, huh-uh! Nah, man! I ain't doin' nothin' while that disgusting thing's in here!" Billy backed himself further into a corner. "Seriously? That stupid thing just squeezed out a wet, juicy dump! Looks like she's got diarrhea! Man, do I seriously gotta clean that up?"

Mr. Bones laughed as he walked over and scooped up the friendly chicken, "This little lady won't hurt you. Here, pet her."

"Pet her? I ain't 'bout to pet no chicken — especially not one that just came in here and deliberately made my job harder!"

"Pet her, Billy... I'm not asking you."

"Why?"

"It's the only way to get used to this place... As a matter of fact, hold out your hands. You're going to hold her."

Billy was ready to die. He couldn't believe his probation officer was taking things to such drastic extremes. Still, he held the chicken for a minute before putting her down and insisting he was ready to get the job done and over with.

Gagging, the teen took the hoe and began scraping dried clumps of manure off of the floor. He had gotten no more than one-fourth of it loose when a mouse literally ran up the wall beside of him.

"Rat, rat, rat!" Billy screamed before running out of the chicken house.

Mr. Bones chuckled while accompanying him back into the coop. "Where? I don't see anything, man."

"It climbed the wall!"

"Really, Billy?... You sure you didn't just see your shadow?"

"I ain't lyin', Mr. Bones! It's probably gonna drop on my head when I ain't lookin'. We gots to be gettin' outta here!"

"It's extremely unusual for a rodent to go up a wall. And I really doubt it's plotting an aerial attack."

"You ain't gonna make me stay in here with that thing?"

"It's gone, Billy... You must have scared it off."

Billy cautiously looked around the building for a moment. "Yeah, well... If he knows what's best for him, he won't be steppin' back up in here. Know what I'm sayin'?"

"Look out!" Mr. Bones hollered, pointing behind Billy's feet. "There he is!"

Billy danced around as if he had already been bitten while squalling and trying to get out the door. Mr. Bones grabbed hold of him, "Get control of yourself, man. It was just a joke."

Billy punched the wall, "Ain't cool, man! Don't do that to me."

"I see why that tiny little mouse wouldn't want to come back up in here," Mr. Bones chuckled. "You'd probably bust his eardrums with all that girly screaming."

"I didn't scream, man!"

"Yeah, whatever. Look, the mouse's probably long gone by now. You can get back to work... Do you need me to stay in here to keep you safe?"

Billy didn't want to be alone with a rat or even a chicken for that matter — unless the chicken was fried sitting next to a pile of mashed potatoes smothered in gravy. At the same time, he had already made himself look like a sissy. Somehow, the boy had to reclaim his dignity. He shook his head, "I ain't afraid of no rat!"

"Good," Mr. Bones replied. "I'll be outside."

Billy had to force himself to breathe as he watched Mr. Bones leave the chicken house. He worked as fast and furiously as possible, determined to get out of that rat-infested place as soon as possible.

It took him longer than he anticipated, but after thirty minutes or so, Billy finally felt confident the coop was clean. "Done!" he announced from the doorway.

Mr. Bones smiled, "Let's have a gander."

Together, the two stepped back inside. "Looking better, but you need to clean the floor under the nesting boxes. Oh, and check out that water bowl — that's as disgusting as all get out!"

"Oh, no!" Billy argued. "You ain't say nothin' 'bout no bowl. I ain't even like cleanin' my own dishes. Definitely ain't up for washin' none that belong to those feathery things."

"I said you have to clean out this pen. The first step is removing the manure off of the floor. Now you get to scrub out their food and watering dishes, take out the old straw, and replace it with new — that should be it for this coop."

How could his probation officer make things sound so simple and pleasant? Billy was certain the guy was laughing on the inside. Probably getting pretty amused at the faces he was making. But maybe not. Maybe he really didn't realize how badly Billy hated this chore. If he didn't know, he was about to find out. "Mr. Bones…," the fourteen-year-old whined, "This is torture!"

"Fifty dollars, man. Fifty dollars you didn't have to steal from anybody. Money you earned from a day's worth of hard labor. Keep telling yourself that."

Billy wasn't complaining about the money, but he had no idea such dirty jobs even existed. "Could you have possibly found something harder for me to do?"

"Oh, I could have! Is that a challenge for next week?"

Billy was glad his probation officer was finding some humor in the situation. Personally, he wished he would have stayed in bed. He didn't even want to imagine what other kind of mess Mr. Bones could get him into. "No, no!" he said. "This is good. Forget I said anything."

By the day's end, Billy was grumbling about how exhausted he was and about his desperate need of a shower. Still, he couldn't help but smile as the property owner handed Mr. Bones the cash.

"Thank you, ma'am," Philip told her.

"Yes, ma'am. Thank you," Billy added.

As they left the grounds, Billy said, "Momma ain't never gonna believe what you made me do."

"She already knows, Billy. We talked about it before I picked you up this morning."

"And she's okay with this?"

"Absolutely. You've been living your life in a self-centered fashion. You never think twice about anybody but yourself. You're going to have to walk a few miles in other people's shoes so you can understand where they're coming from."

"Oh, I get it," Billy said. "So, your little adult feelings got hurt, and now you're getting revenge." He chuckled sarcastically. "That's what that whole sermon thing was about this morning, huh? You told my momma to say mean things about it because I made fun of how short your message was."

"I didn't tell your mother what to say. That was all her," Mr. Bones replied.

Billy knew his mother better than that. She would never have stooped so low had someone not put her up to it. "Liar," he said.

"I'm not lying, Billy. Your mom said whatever came to her mind. I didn't put those thoughts in her head."

"Yeah, whatever!"

"Did it upset you a little there, bud?"

"Oh, no! I loved studyin' for three hours, writin' down a bunch of notes, having my probation officer break into my bedroom and wake me up at the crack of dawn to make me preach him a stupid sermon just so he and my momma could have somethin' to criticize!"

17

Carlos had no desire to check in with his probation officer — not after the last appointment. Too many embarrassing questions. Too much humiliation. Still, he followed his father into the office.

"Please sign in, and I'll let Mr. Bones know you're here," the receptionist told them.

"Thank you," Mr. Estrada replied.

Before they even took their seats, Rose returned and told them they could head back.

Mr. Estrada looked at his thirteen-year-old, "Do you want me to come with you or would you rather I wait out here?"

Carlos didn't understand why his father even asked him that question. He always felt more comfortable with his parents when it came to appointments of any kind. "Come with me," he said.

Mr. Estrada smiled, and the two walked down the short hallway to see Mr. Bones.

The probation officer was typing something up on his computer when they arrived. "Have a seat, gentlemen," he said while opening the Estrada file. "I've received a report from Dr.

Stewart's office. Thank you for following through on the psychological assessment."

"You're most welcome," Mr. Estrada replied.

"So, Carlos… how have things been going, man?"

Carlos felt like the man was out to get him. Like saying the wrong word might land him in the slammer. Pretending to relax, he said, "Good, I guess."

"Has there been any more sexual acting out?"

Carlos shook his head.

"Glad to hear it," Mr. Bones said. "Dad, is that true?"

"As far as I know," Mr. Estrada replied.

"That's the kind of report I like to hear… Carlos, I'm curious… do you have a girlfriend?"

The boy's face reddened as he softly said, "Not anymore."

Mr. Bones couldn't help but chuckle, "A recent break-up, huh? What happened?"

Carlos shook his head, "I'd rather not talk about it."

"Did it have anything to do with those pictures you texted?"

Looking toward the floor, Carlos said, "No."

Mr. Bones stood and rolled his chair out from behind his desk. Sitting closer to the boy, he asked, "Do you get nervous coming here?"

Carlos didn't know what to say. Nervous wasn't really the right word. In all reality, he was horrified. He couldn't just come right out and say that though. Instead, he softly said, "A little."

"Why?"

"Because I don't know you… and I don't like answering personal questions."

"That makes sense… I'll tell you what, bud. I want you to feel more comfortable with me. So, let's move away from the personal questions and get to know each other better. Shall we?"

Carlos felt as if he was being set up. Adults like Mr. Bones always had something up their sleeves. It was a catch twenty-two. If he said he wanted to change the subject, it would look like he was hiding something. If he said he didn't, that would make it easier for the probation officer to continue grilling him about things he would rather keep to himself. Carlos didn't answer. He just looked at the man in silence.

"Let's try this," Mr. Bones said. You can ask me three questions about anything you want. I'll answer them to the best of my ability, and then I'll ask you three, non-personal questions. Deal?"

"Deal." Carlos looked around the office, "Tell me about these trophies. Are they yours?"

"They are," Mr. Bones replied. "When I was in high school, I was a part of a glee club. Do you know what that is?"

"A *geek* club?" Carlos grinned.

"Not geek, Carlos. Glee... It was a group of us who got together and sang short songs; a lot of them were divided up into different parts."

Carlos snickered, "And you got trophies for that?"

"Sure did. Believe it or not, we put a lot of hours into rehearsing. Most of us loved performing. For me, the best part was traveling around to different competitions... Okay, two more questions. What do you have?"

"Hmm...," Carlos said, realizing his first question was way too lame. If his probation officer could ask him personal questions, what was to stop him from turning the tables and giving it back to him? "What's the most humiliating thing you've ever done?" he asked.

Mr. Bones laughed, "Now, that was a good question — not necessarily one I'm going to enjoy answering though."

"Now you know how I feel."

"But I'm going to answer it nonetheless because I'm a man of my word... When I was six years old, I was extremely short for my age. My family went out to eat, and I needed to use the restroom. I insisted I was big enough to go by myself."

Carlos grinned, knowing what was coming next. His probation officer had either missed the toilet and nailed some poor guy's foot, or he slammed the lid on himself.

"Everything was fine until I got the door closed," Mr. Bones continued. "The light switch was up way too high for me. I climbed on top of the toilet seat, and just as I hit the light switch, my foot slipped into the toilet. My pants leg was soaked, and I had to walk back out in the restaurant like that."

Carlos burst out in laughter, "For real? You really did that?... How'd you turn the light back off?"

"I didn't. Just left it on... Okay, last question. What's it going to be?"

Carlos was beginning to enjoy himself. It was nice to see Mr. Bones as just another human being. He wasn't perfect. He was as down-to-earth as anyone else he had ever met. One more question... one more question... what should he ask? It took him a minute, but Carlos finally managed to spit it out, "What kind of trouble did you get into when you were my age?"

Mr. Bones raised an eyebrow, "Somehow, I get the feeling this is a loaded question — but a promise is a promise. So, when I was thirteen... that would put me in what, about seventh grade?"

"Yep."

"Wow, that was probably the worst year of my life. It was the first time I got in a fight."

"Did you kick the guy's butt?"

"Actually, *she* beat the snot out of me."

"You got in a fight with a girl?" Carlos giggled, "And she won?... I would think that would be more embarrassing than falling in the toilet!"

Mr. Bones snickered, "You may have a point there, buddy. But to be completely clear on the matter, I didn't fight back. It's never right to hit a girl, no matter what."

"Yeah," Carlos laughed, "that's probably what I would say too."

"Yeah, yeah," Mr. Bones said. "Well, that was your last question—"

Carlos was a smart little cookie. He saw what was going on. His probation officer didn't like being on the hot seat any more than he did. But, what were his words? Something about a promise being a promise. He was going to make him keep his end of the deal, "You only told me one thing you did. I asked what kinds of things you got in trouble for; not just for one example."

The office phone rang, "Hold on, partner. I have to take this... "Philip Bones speaking... What's he upset about?" Mr. Bones picked up an ink pen and jotted down a few notes. "How long's he been in there?... Do you think he'll talk to me?... Okay... I'll swing by after work. Just don't tell him I'm coming... Thanks, Tamara. See you in a couple of hours... Let me know if anything changes in the meantime.... Sounds good."

After hanging up the phone, Mr. Bones apologized for the interruption. "Now, where were we?"

Mr. Estrada chuckled, "It's okay. You were just about to tell my son more of the naughty things you did when you were his age."

110

JR THOMPSON

"So I was," Mr. Bones smiled. "I'm going to have to move through this fast though so I can have time to ask you some questions. Okay?"

"Sure," Carlos agreed. "As long as you don't try to wiggle your way out of this."

"Wiggle my way out? Why would I do that?"

"Cause you don't want me to know that you did worse things than I did."

Mr. Bones smiled, "Let's see here... I told you about the fight that wasn't really a fight, I, um... well... I sneaked out of the house in the middle of the night—"

"Where'd you go?"

"To a party. Nothing too significant happened there..., I slashed—"

"Nothing significant happened at a party? Come on, Mr. Bones. You have to be honest. Did you drink? Smoke pot? Get a girl pregnant? What happened?"

Mr. Bones shook his head, "I drank a little. But I didn't touch pot, and I didn't get anybody pregnant."

"Boring!" Carlos grinned, "Ok, go on. So, you said you slashed something?"

"I did... the tires on my dad's pickup."

Carlos couldn't help but smile, "And you act like I'm a bad kid... What else did you do?"

"Don't get any bad ideas from this. You understand me?"

Carlos crossed his toes, "Yes, sir."

"I egged my neighbor's house, smoked cigarettes, made prank phone calls, pulled a fire alarm... you name it, I did it."

"Wow, Mr. Bones!... And here I thought you were in a geek club. You were a pretty cool kid."

"Thanks... I think," Mr. Bones replied. "Okay, now I get to ask three questions. For starters, what's the nicest thing you've ever done for somebody?"

Carlos stared at him for a moment. That was not the type of question he had been expecting, "I don't know. That's a tough one."

"Come on, Carlos. We all do nice things for people sometimes. What have you done?"

"Hmm...," he said. "I apologized to an ugly kid in my class for calling him a zit-faced troll... I wouldn't have said I was sorry, but my principal made me. Does that count?"

Mr. Bones chuckled, "If that's the best you can come up with, I guess so. Question number two; if you could change anything about yourself, what would you change and why?"

Carlos shrugged. His dad answered for him, "How about your socks? They could use a good changing!"

Carlos smiled from ear to ear, "Like you can talk... I don't know, Mr. Bones. I can't think of anything."

"Take your time. We're not in any hurry," his probation officer told him.

Carlos looked around the room for a moment, "I guess I would be an adult. That way, I wouldn't have tons of people telling me what to do all of the time."

Mr. Estrada laughed, "Do you not think adults have people tell them what to do, Carlos? I have to listen to my employer, to Mr. Bones here, to our landlord, policemen, the IRS, and a host of other people."

"Yeah, yeah. I still think I'd change myself into an adult. You guys have it made," Carlos said. "What's your next question, Mr. Bones?"

"If you could live anywhere in the world, where would you choose to live and why?"

"That's an easy one! The White House. If I was the President of the United States, I could do anything I want, and nobody could stop me."

18

Tamara hollered for Mr. Bones to come in without bothering to get up.

Mr. Bones let himself in and closed the door behind him, "Still won't come out of his room?"

"Nope."

"So, tell me again what happened."

"I came back from the store and discovered a pair of earrings missing. That boy of mine has done gone out and pawned them. Probably tryin' to get more money for weed."

"And you confronted him?"

"You better believe I did! I waited 'til he came in from school and I tore into him. Told him I can't stand a thieving liar and I ain't gonna put up with it no more. He started givin' me that whole, 'But Momma' spiel. I've seen those puppy-dog eyes far too many times. I ain't buying it this time or ever again for that matter. That boy took my earrings, and he's gonna pay for 'em!"

Mr. Bones was disheartened. Somehow, he had to get Billy's attention. That boy had potential. He could change, but what was it going to take? "And you've tried to get him to come out of his room?"

"Repeatedly. I've beat on that door and screamed so loud my face hurts. At first, he was arguing back at me, but now he's just actin' like I don't exist."

Mr. Bones didn't like the sound of that. It could be that he was ignoring her. It could also mean other things — he could have run away or taken the coward's way out and ended his life. Billy didn't seem the type, but he had been a probation officer long enough to know anything was possible. "Is there any chance he slipped out of his room?" he asked.

"No. I know he's in there. I've heard little sounds here and there. The floor creaking. His bed squeaking... He in there alright."

Mr. Bones thought for a moment. "Tamara, do you trust me?"

"I suppose. Why?"

"Go shopping."

"With what? My good looks? I ain't got no money."

Mr. Bones took out his wallet. "Here's one-hundred bucks. Spend it on whatever you want... well, as long as it's nothing that's going to impair your mind."

"You just gonna go and give me one-hundred dollars?"

"I need some time with Billy."

"Fine by me! Ain't gotta tell me twice... Hey, don't forget what I told you before, Mr. Bones. You can do whatever's necessary. Sometimes I think that boy needs a lot more than a talkin' to if you know what I mean."

"I hear you," Mr. Bones told her. "Why don't you head over to the mall or somewhere? Give us an hour or two."

Tamara stood to her feet. "On my way," she said, grabbing her purse off of the coffee table and heading to the door. "Call if you need me," she said.

"Will do. Thanks," Mr. Bones replied. He watched out the window until Tamara cleared the house. Once she was out of the driveway, he knelt down and whispered a prayer, asking God for wisdom in dealing with Billy.

After a short conversation with his Creator, he went to Billy's door and gave it a light tap. "Billy, it's Mr. Bones... your mother went to the mall for a bit. Can I come in?"

There was no response. Mr. Bones knocked a bit louder. "Billy? Are you okay?"

"Yeah, I'm fine," he mumbled.

"Would you mind unlocking the door for me?"

"You gonna jump on the bandwagon and start accusin' me of stealing from my momma?"

"Billy, I just want to talk, man. I'm not going to leave until I've seen you face-to-face."

"Hold on," he said.

The probation officer relaxed a bit as footsteps came toward the door. Billy unlocked it and walked back to his bed. Mr. Bones opened the door, crossed the room, and sat next to his angry client. "Looks like you've been crying, bud. What's that all about?"

"I ain't been cryin'."

"Why is your pillow wet and why are your eyes so red then?"

"How should I know?"

Mr. Bones had his work cut out for him. That young man had built a wall, and he didn't plan on letting anyone in. "Okay, Billy... why did you lock yourself in your room? What's been going on?"

Stomping his foot, Billy took a deep breath, "Momma done went and started with her accusations again... I tried to tell her but—"

"Billy, look up here at me for a minute."

Billy raised his eyes, "Your mother's earrings are missing. Why would she even think her son might have taken them?"

"I don't know. I guess she just likes to blame people and I's the only one here."

"You don't think it has anything to do with your father's pocket watch?"

"Man, that's old news," Billy retorted, undeniably in defense mode.

"What about the money you recently stole from your mom?"

"See, man! I knew you was gonna do this. Come in here just accusin' me. Nobody ever gives me the chance to defend myself."

Mr. Bones could understand where his probationer was coming from. But the kid wasn't seeing the bigger picture. "Billy, right now I'm not talking about the earrings. I'm referring to your character."

"Who cares about my character? I'm sick and tired of getting blamed for everything! I ain't do nothin', Mr. B!"

"Did you sell your daddy's pocket watch?"

"Yeah, and I'm sorry for that."

"Did you steal some cash from your mother?"

"Yeah, and I know that was wrong too."

"Billy, when you make a habit of being dishonest, people are always going to jump to the conclusion that you're responsible when something comes up missing."

Billy shook his head, "That ain't right, Mr. B. Ain't never right to be accusin' somebody without no evidence."

"Where'd your momma get those earrings?"

"Daddy bought 'em for her on their anniversary — the last one they celebrated together before he died."

"Billy, Billy, Billy..." Mr. Bones sighed. "Do you have hard feelings toward your old man?"

The fourteen-year-old leaped to his feet. "I did not... steal... any... stupid... earrings!" he shouted with a tear trickling down his face. "I wouldn't do that... not after seeing how much it hurt my momma when I took the watch."

"Then where are they, Billy?"

"Finally!" the young man growled. "It's about time somebody'll give me a chance to talk. I kept trying to tell Momma, but she won't listen. No, she done has her mind made up. She—"

"Where are they, Billy?"

"She let one of her girlfriends borrow 'em about a month ago."

Mr. Bones raised an eyebrow, "You're sure of this?"

"Absolutely! Call Janice and ask her. I'm sure Momma's got her number written down here someplace."

"No need for that, bud. Sit back down here for me."

Billy took a seat, and Mr. Bones gave him a hug from the side. "I believe you, son. Thank you for telling the truth."

Billy half-smiled, "You gonna talk to my momma about this?"

"Yes, sir. I will. But Billy... locking yourself in your room isn't a very good idea."

"Why ain't it? You think I should've just sat down here and let her keep nagging me 'bout somethin' I ain't do?"

Mr. Bones knew where the boy was coming from. He had been in his shoes many times. He had also seen how that way of thinking had destroyed many good men over the years.

"What's going to happen someday when you get married? You and your wife are going to have some disagreements, bud. You have to learn to talk things out. Sometimes you have to allow someone else to vent their frustrations and their feelings before you get a chance to say anything back. But eventually... if you wait patiently, you'll get your turn to speak. I don't want to hear about you giving your momma the silent treatment anymore. Do you understand me?"

Billy sat silently for a few seconds before saying, "Yeah man, I got you."

19

"Good morning," Rose said as Philip entered the main office.

Philip nodded and continued toward his private domain.

"Wait a second," she interrupted.

Philip couldn't help but notice his secretary's mischievous grin. "What's up?"

"Oh, nothing much. Just thought I'd let you know my niece is in town this weekend. You guys are about the same age, and I was wondering if—"

Philip knew where that conversation was headed. "I don't do blind dates," he said coldly.

"She's a cutie. Can I at least show you her picture?"

"Nah, that's okay," Philip replied. "I have a lot on my plate right now."

"But Philip... Listen... Kelly's a pediatrician, she loves kids, she's a Sunday School teacher." Rose's smile was larger than any Philip had ever seen her wear. "You two would be perfect together."

Philip shook his head. "I'm not interested but show me her picture, Rose."

Giggling with joy, Rose motioned for Philip to walk around her desk. As he came around, she pointed to her computer screen, "Isn't she gorgeous?"

Philip was impressed. Gorgeous was an understatement. Wavy blonde hair, welcoming blue eyes, thin lips... he tried to keep his eyes from widening. He didn't want Rose to have a clue how that picture was speaking to his heart. He didn't speak until he was sure he could mask his true feelings. "Not too bad," he said.

"I told her about you," Rose replied. "She asked a lot of questions — I bet she'd say yes if you invited her out for dinner."

Philip shook his head. He had been down that road too many times before. "Not this time, Rose. I'm going to have to pass."

"But Philip," his secretary whined, "she's only going to be in this one weekend. I don't know how long it might be before she passes through again."

"No, Rose. The answer is no. I don't have time for a date this weekend."

"Oh, Philip! No wonder Cassie broke up with you!" She minimized her screen, "There is more to life than just working with troubled kids. You need to get out some."

"First of all, I'd appreciate it if you didn't bring Cassie into this. Secondly, Rose, I've got to get my files. I have a few schools to visit this morning."

"I know you do... When should I expect you to return?"

Philip looked at his watch. "Um... I'd say no later than noon. I have a couple of probationers coming by after lunch."

"Sounds good. If you change your mind about my niece, let me know as soon as possible, okay?"

"Sure, Rose. I'll give it some thought, but don't hold your breath."

Philip grabbed a few files and rushed out of the office before Rose could corner him again. It was going to be another busy day.

His first stop was Westview Middle School. Mr. Ponderosa caught him coming in the door. "Morning, Mr. Bones. Swinging by to check on Alden?"

"I am... How have things been going?"

Mr. Ponderosa grinned, "I haven't heard any reports on him as of late, so I'm going to assume no news is good news. If you want to check in at the office, you're welcome to go around and speak with his teachers. You have a copy of his schedule, right?"

"Sure do... Thanks, Mr. Ponderosa."

Philip checked in with all seven of Alden's teachers and received nothing but glowing reviews. Finally, he was beginning to feel like he had made an impact on the young man's life.

As he left the school, Philip's cell phone startled him. Whipping it out of his pocket, he glanced at the caller id — it was the office. "Philip speaking," he answered.

"Philip, this is Rose. Honey, I've got some bad news for you. I'm getting sick to my stomach. I don't know if it's the flu or what."

"Sorry to hear that, Rose," Philip said, somewhat disappointed. He should have been used to it. Things never went as expected — not in his line of work. "Can you stay there until I get back to the office?"

"I can try... But I can't stick around much longer."

"On my way," Philip said. He hated the thoughts of the office being empty. Oh, the joys of a two-person department.

In no time, he was back at the courthouse. Rose met him at the door, "Philip, I'd like you to meet somebody."

The probation officer shook his head, "I should have known... Let me guess, Kelly, right?"

"This is Kelly. It's not what you think, Philip... I asked her to pick me up because I'm not feeling well."

Kelly was even more beautiful in person than she was in her picture. Philip forced himself to keep his eyes off of her. "You mean so she and I would have a chance to see each other?" he asked.

Rose smiled, "Now, Philip, would I ever do such a thing?"

Kelly grinned from ear to ear. "Nice to meet you," she said.

"You as well," Philip replied. With a wink, he added, "I would certainly hate to keep your aunt waiting with her getting sick and all... You might want to take her to the doctor in case it's anything serious."

"I'm sure it's not that bad," Rose interjected. "I need some rest; that's all. And besides, if it's anything serious, Kelly is a physician."

"Right," Philip said. "I remember you telling me that. Well, I will let you two ladies be getting on your way now."

With that, Philip walked past them and headed to his office, still shaking his head. He had to admit, if only to himself, that Kelly appeared to be a sweet girl and he could see himself with her — but it was too soon. He was not about to go out with anyone while there was even a slight chance he was on the rebound.

The office phone rang a few minutes after Rose's departure. "Probation officer Philip Bones speaking," he answered.

It was someone trying to reach the adult parole office. Philip gave her the correct number.

"Can you connect me, please? I've already tried calling over there three times; I keep getting through to wrong departments."

Philip hated that question. He didn't mind transferring people to any other department in the building. But that one? Why? Concealing his frustration, Philip said, "No problem," before dialing the extension himself and waiting for the receptionist to pick up.

The phone rang four times. "Cassie speaking."

Cassie? She wasn't supposed to answer. She never answered. What was this? Was there a secret secretary party going on somewhere? "Hey Cassie, this is Philip."

"What do you want?"

"I have a client on the line who says she can't get through to your office. Can I pass her through?"

"In a minute... First, I have a question for you."

Philip's curiosity was aroused, "What's that?"

"I know you're probably the wrong person to ask but how soon do you think is too soon?"

"Too soon for what?"

Cassie giggled in a way he hadn't heard her giggle in a long time, "An engagement."

Philip thought his eyes were going to pop out of his head. "You're kidding me! The guy asked you to marry him already?"

"No," Cassie giggled. "I'm thinking about asking him."

Philip pushed his chair back away from his desk. "You're what?... Cassie... really?"

"Why not?"

"Whatever floats your boat, I guess," Philip said. "But I can tell you this much. Had you asked me to marry you, I would've run the other way."

"Why?"

"Cassie, we have a client waiting to be transferred. We're both being unprofessional right now."

"Fine. Send her through," Cassie groaned. "I'll call you later."

20

There came the knock Billy had been dreading. 6:00 in the morning was way too early to get up on a Saturday. But the teenager knew Mr. Bones was a persistent man, and there was no way he could get out of it.

The probation officer knocked again before Billy's eyelids popped open. "I'm up," the sluggish young man groaned. "Be out in a minute."

"Good," Mr. Bones replied. "Don't fall back asleep."

"I won't," Billy mumbled, slowly sitting up and glancing out the window. He could only hope he wasn't going to be working in any chicken coops. Climbing out of bed, he got dressed.

Just as he was tying his second shoe, Mr. Bones pounded on the door again. "You didn't go back to sleep, did you, boy?"

"No. I'm getting my shoes on. Momma got breakfast ready yet?"

"Yeah, man. There's some cinnamon flavored oatmeal out there with your name on it."

Billy thought he was going to gag. "She did that on purpose! Momma knows I hate oatmeal."

"Regardless, you're going to eat it. Your mother didn't get up early and prepare that food for me, you know."

"I'll eat it," Billy moaned as he came to the door. "So, what we gonna be workin' on today?"

"You'll find out."

"How much it pay?"

"I'll tell you later. Let's get in that kitchen and eat some breakfast... and don't go in there with an attitude."

Billy shook his head, "Fine, but I ain't gonna like it."

When they got to the kitchen, Tamara quickly told her son good morning, then, with a yawn, announced she was going back to bed. Mr. Bones and Billy ate their breakfast in silence.

As soon as they were through, the probation officer made Billy wash the dishes and clean up the kitchen. Billy still didn't speak a word.

Putting the last dish in the cabinet, he said, "Now what?"

"Now, we head to the work site."

Somehow that didn't make Billy feel any better. "We goin' to that same lady's house we went to last weekend?"

"Nope. Brand new weekend, brand new assignment."

"What we gonna be doin'?"

"You'll see... Do you have any work gloves?"

Billy didn't like the sound of that. "Work gloves?" he repeated.

"Don't worry about it. I brought an extra pair along. Let's go. Mr. Davis is expecting us."

Billy put his hands in his pockets, "Let's do this then."

The two walked out to the car and rushed off to Alan Davis's place. Billy was surprised to see how young the guy was. He guessed he was in his early twenties, if that.

"I had them unload the wood out back; I've got a splitting maul and an axe back there," the man told Mr. Bones. "I appreciate what you're doing for this boy by the way."

"And I appreciate you giving him this opportunity," Mr. Bones replied.

Billy had heard enough about who appreciated who for doing what. He had his own ideas as to what they ought to be talking about. "How much this job pay?" he asked.

"Seventy-five dollars, man," Mr. Davis replied.

"Alright. I'm down with that... How long you expect me to work?"

"Depends on how fast you bust through that pile of wood," Mr. Bones interjected.

Billy half-expected that answer. There was no point in seeking clarification. When his probation officer was in that mood, he wasn't about to let Mr. Davis provide any additional information, and Billy knew it. "Great," he said. "Let's get this show on the road then."

Mr. Bones led his probationer to the back of the house. Billy's eyes widened at the sight of an enormous stack of firewood — it was roughly ten feet high and somewhere around twenty feet in diameter. "What am I supposed to do with this?"

"Have you ever split firewood?" Mr. Bones asked.

"Split wood?... No... But ain't no need to do that here anyway. Looks like it's done been cut."

"The trees have been sawed into smaller logs, but now they have to be split. Here, let me show you how it's done." Mr. Bones pulled out a large block of wood and set a smaller one on top of it. He raised the maul above his head, "It's pretty simple, Billy. Watch and learn." He brought the splitting maul down hard and fast.

Seeing the block of wood split in two, Billy couldn't help but smile. "Looks easy enough," he said.

Mr. Bones held the maul out to him, "Hold this for a second while I get another log ready."

Billy took in a few deep breaths while waiting his turn. "Okay, bud. I want you to stand with your feet apart, like this. That way, if you miss the log, you're not going to slice your ankles."

The fourteen-year-old took offense to that statement. Cocking his head, he said, "You sayin' I'm clumsy, Mr. B.?"

"No, sir. Just trying to prevent any possibility of injuries... You put your right hand on the upper part of the handle and your left hand on the lower end."

Billy complied.

"Yeah, just like that. Now you're going to aim for the center of that block of wood."

Billy brought the blade down nice and slow, raised it up, and repeated the process a few times.

"Good," Mr. Bones told him. "Now swing with everything you've got."

Billy put so much effort into concentrating on that wood that his breathing nearly stopped. He swung but over-extended the handle to the point it connected with the firewood, jarring the teen's shoulder. Billy dropped the splitting maul, "Ah, man!"

"It's okay, Billy. That's how you learn. Pick it up and try again."

The next four swings were equally as unsuccessful. Billy wiped the sweat from his forehead. He was ready to call it a day. "I can't do this," he whined. "This be white man's work. Do I look white to you?"

"There's no such thing as white man's work. Anybody can do this. It just takes practice. Try it again but this time, zero in on it. Don't be feeble with your swing."

Billy raised the splitting maul again while giving his probation officer a dirty look. Pretending that block of wood was the skull of Mr. Bones, he brought the maul down with more power and precision than he thought possible; the log broke into three pieces.

"One down, about five-hundred more to go," Mr. Bones teased.

"I got this," Billy said, grabbing another piece of wood and getting it in position. He tried the same technique, but it was a fail. The maul went into the block but got stuck.

Mr. Bones had to get it out for him. "Again, Billy," he insisted.

Time and time again, Billy erred but eventually got the hang of splitting wood. After splitting ten pieces or so, Mr. Bones gave him a lesson in properly stacking the chopped wood in a neat, orderly fashion. "This will help the wood season before Mr. Davis throws it in his fireplace."

Billy looked confused. "Season? What you mean?"

"Right now, this wood has a lot of sap in it. If Mr. Davis burns it as it is, that sap will cause creosote build-up in his chimney, and it'll be a fire danger. Once the wood is split, the air can get to it better and dry it out."

"Gotcha," Billy said. "But Mr. B, I don't think I'm gonna be able to get all this done today. My back's already killing me. And look at my hands!"

Mr. Bones took a look. "Way to go, Billy! You got yourself some first-rate callouses forming there. Why aren't you wearing those gloves I gave you?"

Billy shrugged, "Guess I forgot."

"I bet you won't forget before you split anymore, will you?"

Billy shook his head, "No, sir. I sure won't!"

For five excruciating hours, Billy worked and complained but not necessarily in that order. He couldn't wait to get home. The teenager was looking forward to getting his six weeks of Saturday work completed and picking up some hard-earned cash.

21

Billy couldn't believe it. Every time something came up missing, he was the first one people wanted to point their fat little fingers at. It was bad enough when it was his momma, but two of his teachers ganging up on him at school like that — making him empty his pockets, checking the contents of his locker, and not even apologizing when they didn't find anything. Huh-uh! He wasn't about to put up with that. No, sir!

When Billy was instructed to go back to class, he left the office alright — and marched straight out the front door. It wasn't like he enjoyed being there anyway. For the first few blocks, the teen frequently looked over his shoulder to make sure he hadn't been followed.

He saw a couple of guys playing basketball. "Hey man," one of them called out. "Wanna shoot some hoops?"

"Some other time," Billy said, continuing his walk to a destination that remained a mystery even to himself.

Less than two minutes passed before a lady with messed up hair and a few missing teeth emerged from an alley. "Can you help a sister out with some pocket change?"

"Ain't got none," Billy replied.

"Man, you didn't even check those pockets! Surely, you got something. Hey, I'll even settle for a joint. Got one?"

"I ain't got nothin' I told you."

"Seriously?" the woman shouted in disgust. "What's wrong with you? Can't even help a woman in need!"

"I would help if I could, Miss, but I got enough problems of my own."

She placed her hands on her hips while simultaneously rolling her eyes, "Like what?"

"Talkin' 'bout it ain't gonna do no good," Billy said, crossing the street.

She followed him. "Come on, my brother! Open up and tell me all about it. Who knows? Maybe I can help."

The stalking drug-addict was quickly getting under his skin. Billy felt like strangling her. "Would you leave me alone?"

Smiling, she playfully said, "Sure… If you give me your wallet."

Billy turned to face her. "My wallet?… It's empty."

"If that's the case, what do you have to lose? I can keep following you and your cute self around town, or you can give it to me, and I'll let you be on your way."

Billy walked closer to her, "I ain't afraid of you!"

"What you gonna do?" she shouted. "Hit a girl?"

"If I have to!" Billy retorted.

Another woman shot out of an alley. "Sissy, leave that boy alone!" she screamed. "I'm sorry, sir… My sister's higher than a kite; when she gets like this—"

"I ain't high!"

"Go, boy. I'll take care of her."

Taking advantage of the distraction, Billy got himself out of there in record time. Rounding a bend, he saw a vehicle that looked all too familiar. "Momma?" he said out loud as he watched her car coming to a halt.

"Get your behind in this car right now!" she demanded.

Billy thought about running. To give himself more time to decide, he tried a stall tactic. "Momma, how'd you know I was out here?"

"Cause Momma knows these things and don't you ever forget it! I got eyes all over the place!"

That answer was not one unfamiliar to the fourteen-year-old. He looked toward the ground, shook his head, and lightly kicked at the sidewalk.

"Did I not tell you to get in this car?" Tamara screamed.

Billy took a deep breath, got in, and slumped down in the passenger seat.

Tamara pulled out, "Why ain't you in school?"

"I'm sick of it, Momma! Everybody always makin' allegations against me!"

Tamara looked at him through the corner of her eye, "Billy, what did you do this time?"

"See what I mean, Momma?... You know what! Why don't you just call Mr. Bones and tell him to put me in juvie? That way everybody'll know I ain't stealin' nothin' from nobody!"

"I can do better than that, son. Let's just stop in at the courthouse and see if he's in his office. I can't take any more of this either. I can't follow around after you all of the time like you're a two-year-old!"

"Good, Momma! Take me over there then... Maybe together we can talk some sense into the man."

Tamara wasn't playing. She drove straight to the courthouse. Even when she parked the car, Billy couldn't tell if she was calling his bluff or if she meant it, but he got out anyway. His momma followed close behind.

Mr. Bones was on his way out of the building when they got to the door. "We didn't have an appointment today, did we?" he asked.

"No, but you better make time for one," Tamara shouted. "Somethin's got to give!"

"I'm actually headed to one of the schools. I have a situation I have to deal with."

"It looks like that other situation's just gonna have to wait! This young man needs his probation revoked. He wants it to happen, and so do I!"

"Is this true, Billy?"

At that point, Billy had given up on life. He had a bad reputation, and no matter what he did, it wasn't going to change any time in the near future. "Yes, sir," he said. "I'd rather be behind bars than have everybody makin' allegations against me all the time."

Mr. Bones looked disappointed, "I don't really have time to deal with this right now. Can I give you a call in about an hour?"

"An hour?" Tamara scoffed. "What am I supposed to do with him for an hour?"

"Billy, if your momma takes you back to the house, will you promise me you'll do whatever she tells you to do?"

"Yeah, sure."

"Good... Tamara, take him home and work him half to death until you hear from me."

Billy threw his hands up in the air. "What?... That ain't right, Mr. B! You ain't even know what's going on."

"I know that I don't have time for this right now. Tamara, I'm sure you have a toilet or two that needs scrubbed, some garbage to be taken out, a cobweb or two knocked down?"

"Oh, I can keep him busy alright."

Billy stomped the ground, "I ain't gonna—"

"You already promised you'd do whatever your mother tells you to do," Mr. Bones reminded him.

"Yeah, but this ain't what *she's* telling me to do. It's what *you're* telling me to do."

"I'm just giving your mother advice. What she tells you is completely up to her... I've got to go, folks. I'll get in touch as soon as I possibly can. But I have an emergency to deal with."

"Thanks," Tamara said. "I'll be expecting your call."

"Yeah, thanks a lot, Mr. B. We appreciate it," Billy said sarcastically.

"Come on, young man," Tamara snapped. Grabbing his arm, she said, "We've got things to do!"

Jutting his lip out, Billy dragged his feet back to the car. First his teachers, then the principal, then his own momma, and now his probation officer. He wanted to close his eyes and never wake up again.

Tamara turned the radio up full blast. Billy knew that was out of character for her, but he didn't utter a word. He just stared out the window until they got to the house. As they pulled into the driveway, Tamara turned the music off. "We ain't gonna be havin' no conversations 'til we hear from your probation officer. You hear me?"

"Yes, Momma."

"Good... In the meantime, we gonna be honoring his suggestions. You gonna start with that nasty restroom. I want it to shine. The toilet, the tub, the sink, the mirror, the floor—"

"I get it, Momma."

"You better or you're liable to get somethin' else! When you get finished with that bathroom, you'll go into the laundry room and get the clothes out of the dryer. Fold 'em neatly and put 'em away. If there's any time left after that, I want you to scrub down the walls in the entryway."

Billy shook his head.

"What's that supposed to mean?" His momma yelled. "You promised to do whatever I say!"

"I'm gonna keep my promise, Momma. It's just that none of this is fair. I—"

"Did I not make myself clear? We are not gonna be havin' no conversations right now! You get in there and get to work!"

Billy got out of the car and shut his door roughly.

"Don't you be slammin' doors or I'll make you work all night! Do you understand me?"

"Sorry, Momma."

"Not as sorry as you're gonna be if it happens again!"

If there was one chore Billy despised more than any other, it was cleaning toilets. He wouldn't mind if he was the only one who used it but his house only had one restroom. The thoughts of who else had touched that seat and what they had dropped in that bowl... it just didn't seem right that he had to clean it up.

Billy closed the restroom door and flushed the toilet five times — making sure the water was as clean as possible. Squinting his eyes and looking as though he had just bit into a lemon, he grabbed the toilet brush and began scrubbing. He worked on that bathroom so long he lost track of time. Just as he bagged up the trash, his momma hollered, "Billy, your probation officer's on the phone!"

The teen flung the door open. "So? What you want me to do about it?"

"He wants to talk to you."

"So?"

"Get down here and talk to the man, right now!"

Glancing down at the floor, Billy grumbled, "On my way, Momma."

The boy was upset because he already knew where his conversation with Mr. Bones was going to go — and he was right too. His probation officer told him it was his own fault nobody trusted him. If he didn't steal, he wouldn't be thought of as a thief. If he didn't lie, his integrity wouldn't be taken into question. If he didn't skip school, he wouldn't be hunted down by an angry momma bear.

"So, what we gonna do, Mr. B? I gonna move into a cell down at Juvie?"

"No, Billy, you're not. I believe that's exactly what you want to happen. I had a talk with your momma. In addition to your work days, you're going to start attending church with me on Wednesday evenings."

"What? You can't make me do that!"

"Oh, yes I can! Your momma's all for it. You'll be expected to bring a notebook and an ink pen so you can take notes. I'm going to quiz you after the services to see what you're learning."

"Come on, Mr. B!... Why?"

"You skipped class, Billy. You should have been at school learning something. The punishment fits the crime. Now you'll go to school like you're supposed to and do some extra learning one evening per week as well."

22

Philip tried to refocus his mind, but it was difficult. The Gallagher's had just left his office with their daughter, Angel. Even though Angel should have been named Demon, her parents were the perfect portrait of love. Every time they came in, their faces were glowing, they were holding hands with their fingers interlocked, and some mild flirtation was going on between them.

Philip remembered when he and Cassie used to be that close. He still couldn't believe things hadn't worked out between them. She was the only one he had ever imagined spending the rest of his life with. Some of her criticisms hade made themselves a permanent nest in his brain. To a certain degree, she was right. How was Philip ever going to have time for a relationship with anyone? Eight-hour work days, evenings and weekends spent mentoring youths or attending church services, and sleeping — that was his life in a nutshell. There wasn't time for anything else.

Rose tapped on the door, "Sorry to bother you, Philip; Judge Hastings just called. He had to reschedule the appointment you have at 3:00 this afternoon."

"Wonderful," Philip said. "Thanks for letting me know."

"That's what I'm here for."

Removing the Ramsey file from his desk, Philip placed it back in the file cabinet. "Well, that's one thing off my list today," he muttered.

Rose tapped on the door again. "Philip, I'm sorry, but I forgot to deliver this. It was dropped off here this morning for you."

Philip took the envelope out of her hand and opened it up. "Are you kidding?"

"What is it?" Rose asked.

"Cassie's getting married and she invited me to her wedding!"

Rose's jaw dropped in disbelief.

"It's her life," Philip said. "But I'm declining the invitation."

"Can't say I blame you," Rose said before leaving Philip to his stack of paperwork.

Philip shook his head. He had heard of people going on the rebound and of ex's attempting to make their former boyfriends jealous, but Cassie didn't seem the type. Was she seriously ready to wreck her life just to hurt his feelings?

The office phone rang. "Philip Bones speaking."

"Mr. Bones, it's me, Tamara."

"Uh-oh," the probation officer said. "What's going on?"

"Billy's not going to be coming to the service this evening."

Mr. Bones sighed. "Why? Is he sick?"

"No, nothing like that. I just have some errands I need to run, and he asked if he can tag along with me."

"Tamara, we had an agreement. We have to work together as a team or Billy isn't going to straighten up."

"He's doing much better today. It's like he's a whole new kid. He'll be fine."

The probation officer's heart sank. He knew exactly where this was going to lead and it wasn't going to be pretty. "Tamara, if this blows up in your face, you can only blame yourself. That boy needs to know he can't snake his way out of consequences."

"Well... personally, I don't think church ought to be seen as a consequence anyway."

Mr. Bones cleared his throat. "Tamara, you're making this very difficult. How can I help you with Billy if you keep interfering?"

"Me interfering? He's my son! You're the outsider here! Not me!"

"Okay, Tamara. Feel free to get in touch if you need me."

"I'll keep that in mind... but really, I think he'll be fine."

"I hope you're right," Mr. Bones said. "Enjoy your afternoon."

"You too."

Hanging up the phone, Philip slapped his desk. Bowing his head, he prayed, "Heavenly Father, I don't know what it is about this day, but nothing is going as planned. I'm frustrated and need a breath of fresh air. Lord, please do something to loosen the tension. I know you don't owe me anything—"

Rose tapped on the door.

"Yes," Philip replied.

"I know you're probably ready to kill me by now. I'm just having one of those days... Somehow this other envelope had gotten mixed up in a batch of papers on my desk."

"Another one?... From Cassie?"

"Nope."

"From who then?"

"Oh, just open it."

Thinking about his prayer, Philip nervously opened the envelope. Inside was a letter and three quarters:

> Dear Mr. Bones,
>
> Thank you for giving me so many chances. I'm not very good at saying thank you in person, but I am thankful for everything you've done for me. I miss hanging out on the island with you, and I hope we can do that again soon.
>
> Thanks,
> Alden
>
> P.S.
> I hope this will cover the cost of that ice cream I wasted the first time you picked me up after school.

That was just what Philip needed! A smile blossomed on his face. Picking up the phone, he called Mrs. Wamboldt's cell phone. "Hi, this is Philip Bones, Alden's probation officer. Is he with you by any chance?"

"He sure is... Hold on a second."

"Thank you."

Philip waited patiently for a moment before hearing a cheerful, "Hi, Mr. Bones... Did your secretary give you my note?"

"She sure did. That made my day, Alden!"

"Awesome! I wish I could do more, but those three quarters were all the money I had to my name."

"That's okay, man. Always be willing to go the extra mile to show somebody you appreciate them. That will get you a long way in life. Hey... what are you doing this evening?"

"Homework. Why?"

"Do you want to go to church with me?"

"Hold on. Let me ask Grandma... Grandma, Mr. Bones wants to know if I can go to church with him in a little while!... Can I?..."

There was a brief pause before Alden got back to him. "She said I can. Does she need to bring me to your place or are you going to pick me up?"

"I'll be by around 6:00. Will that work?"

"Sounds great. Thanks, Mr. Bones."

"You're welcome! And thank you again."

23

Bright and early Saturday morning Mr. Bones knocked on Billy's bedroom door, "Time to get up, man!"

The teen didn't respond.

Mr. Bones knocked louder. "It's 6:00, Billy. We have work to do, and your mother has breakfast on the table."

Still no answer.

"How late did he stay up last night?" Mr. Bones hollered toward the kitchen.

"I don't know. He was still up when I went to bed."

"Wonderful," the probation officer said. He let himself into the room, only to find it empty.

Mr. Bones was furious but he should have known. "He's not here, Tamara! Any idea where he might be?"

She shook her head. "That boy, I don't know what to do with him sometimes."

"You should not have allowed him to bail on church Wednesday night. Now, he thinks you're always going to get him out of any consequences he has coming to him."

Tamara raised an eyebrow, "Oh, so now it's my fault he's a teenager? Come on, Mr. Bones! Teenagers do crazy things.

We all know that. It ain't nobody's fault. He probably went out to a party or somethin'."

"And that's okay with you? It doesn't bother you to think that your fourteen-year-old boy may have gotten drunk and got himself into who knows what kind of trouble last night?"

"As long as he ain't stealin', vandalizin' nothing, hurtin' people, or bringing drugs up in here, I ain't got no problem with it. Boys will be boys."

"Tamara, do you care about your son's future?"

"Of course I do!"

"Than you can't continue allowing him to do whatever he pleases. It's illegal for a boy his age to be out drinking. Not to mention, he violated his probation by not abiding by his curfew."

"Lock him up then!"

"People ought to be required to have a license before they can have children," Mr. Bones mumbled.

"You know what? You have outstayed your welcome, Mr. Bones. Get out of my house!"

"Thanks for giving me permission," Mr. Bones retorted before nearly stomping out and slamming the door. He couldn't stand it when a negligent parent undermined his authority with their teenagers like Tamara had done. It made his job ten times more difficult than it needed to be.

As Mr. Bones started his car and headed for home, he tried to decide what steps to take next. Billy was showing little to no signs of improvement, and his mother was only adding to the boy's problems. Approaching his driveway, he caught sight of Billy lounging on his doorstep. The young man got up and cautiously approached.

"Where have you been?" Mr. Bones demanded.

"Out."

"Out where?"

"What's it to you? Look, man. I'm keeping my end of the bargain. I'm here and ready to work. Ain't that all that matters?"

"You violated your probation."

"How?"

"By being out after curfew."

"Ah, it ain't no big thing, Mr. B. I didn't break no laws or nothin'."

"Were you drinking?"

Billy shook his head.

"Smoking pot?"

"No, man! I ain't into that no more."

"Where were you then?"

"Do you seriously expect me to tell you about my love life?"

Mr. Bones looked toward the sky. "Tell me you didn't? Billy, you're way too young for that. What if you set yourself up to be a daddy? You have no way to support a child. No way to put a roof over his head. No way to put food in his belly."

"Mr. B, a girl don't get pregnant just having sex with her one time."

"Believe it or not, that can happen. But there's more to it than that... You could get an incurable disease."

"What is with you, man? Momma don't care if I stay out late. She don't care what I do with my personal life. What's it to you?"

"I care about you, Billy."

"And you're saying Momma don't?"

Mr. Bones shook his head, "No, I'm not saying that. I can't speak for your mother. All I can speak for is myself. I don't want to see you get hurt or strap yourself down financially for the rest of your life. Wait until you're an adult and you have a career… get married… and then have children. That's the way God intended it to be."

"Yeah, well… I'll think about it. Shouldn't we get going now?"

Mr. Bones let out an annoyed sigh, turned, and got back in the car. Billy hopped in the passenger side, and they drove to the Ingall's place without speaking another word.

When they entered the driveway, Mr. Bones smirked. "I guess you can see you've got your work cut out for you today, huh?"

Billy's eyes widened as he looked at the disaster in front of him. The yard was full of soda cans, potato chip bags, scraps of food, broken buckets, and every other kind of garbage one could imagine.

"The Ingall family just purchased this place and have generously agreed to pay you $100 to clean up the property."

"$100? Mr. B., you know anybody else would charge at least $500 for this!"

"You're not anybody else, are you?"

"Really? This ain't fair, Mr. B! How you be findin' these people?"

"Would you please stop calling me Mr. B?... I feel like I tell you about this at least once a week!"

24

Wednesday afternoon Mr. Bones stopped by Billy's school to check in on him. On his way to the office, he ran into the teen in the hallway. "Afternoon, Mr. Bones," Billy said.

"Good to see you, Billy. Hope I get a good report on you."

"You will, sir. Hey… sorry for bailin' on you last week at church. Do you want me to come tonight?"

"I'd love that, man."

"Well, I've been givin' it some thought. I believe you really do care about me and it wasn't right to manipulate Momma into letting me skip last week. I've made a lot of mistakes, Mr. Bones and I apologize for that." The bell rang. "Gotta get to class. Don't want to be late," Billy said.

"Good plan. Swing by my office after school, will you?"

"Yes, sir."

For once, Philip received a positive report on Billy. Other than the recent incident of walking out over the theft allegation, his teachers had nothing negative to say about his behavior or attitude.

Philip knew the boy was far from being out of the woods, but it sounded like something was finally getting through his thick skull.

After stopping at two other schools to check on other students, Philip made his way back to the office. Rose smiled as he walked through the door. "What's that look for?" Philip asked.

"What look?"

"You know what look."

Giggling, Rose said, "I scheduled an appointment for you."

"With who?"

"They're waiting in your office. You showed up just when I thought you would."

"You left a client in my office? Do you realize how much trouble we can get into if they snooped through any of my files?"

"I'm sure that's not a problem. But you might want to head back there. I'm sure you don't want to keep your appointment waiting."

Philip didn't know what to expect as he walked down the hall but he hoped it was a client and not Rose's niece. The last thing he wanted to do was go on a blind date. He had already made that clear though. Surely, Rose wouldn't start matchmaking again. Besides, Kelly should no longer be in town.

Entering his office, Philip locked eyes on a man he had never seen before. His visitor was dressed in a suit and tie and had taken a seat across from his desk. "Hello, sir," Philip said.

"Mr. Bones?"

"Yes, sir... And who might you be?"

"My name's Danny Michaels; I'm the head deacon at Freedom Baptist Church."

"Nice to meet you, Brother Michaels. How can I help you?"

"Mr. Bones, our pastor passed away a couple of months ago. We've been making do the best we can without a leader, but we really need someone to fill the pulpit regularly. We've made a lot of phone calls, and it's our understanding that you've recently been called to preach."

Philip shook his head, "I'm not ready to be a pastor."

Brother Michaels laughed, "Nor are you qualified to be one. You're still a novice, and you're not yet the husband of one wife."

Philip didn't know what to think of that response. It was obvious the man had done his research anyway. "Uh, okay," he replied. "Why are you here then?"

"We were wondering if you would like some additional speaking opportunities?"

Philip chuckled nervously, "Sure... I guess I can handle that."

"Every Sunday we have two morning services, and a preaching hour in the evenings; on Wednesday nights we come together for a prayer service... What can you commit to?"

Philip chuckled again, "I don't know. This is kind of sudden... What do you have in mind?"

"The more you can preach for us, the happier we'll be."

Philip pulled up the calendar on his phone and examined it for a moment. "I believe I can handle the evening services for a while but the mornings might be a too much right now."

"That's understandable," Brother Michaels said. "Here, let me give you my phone number... Call me after work this evening, and I'll give you directions to the church."

"Sounds like a plan. Thank you for the opportunity, sir."

After the deacon left his office, Philip whispered a prayer of thanksgiving and asked God for the wisdom to take on the task that had been placed before him.

As soon as he finished praying, Rose tapped on the door. "Andrea Fisher is here for a check in."

"Thanks, Rose. Send her back."

Philip got in his file cabinet and pulled out the girl's folder. Just as he opened it up, Andrea walked in with a strange expression on her face. "Why were you talking to Danny?"

"Danny?"

"Yeah, the guy who just left your office."

"You know him?"

"Yeah, he goes to my church."

The probation officer laughed. "I didn't know you go to church, Andrea."

"Now you do... What was he doing here?"

"He asked if I could fill the pulpit for a while."

Andrea gave him a dirty look. "You said no, right?"

Mr. Bones shook his head.

"So now I'm going to be seeing you here, at school, and at church? That's slightly obsessive, don't you think?"

Mr. Bones didn't know what to make of the situation. It was obvious Andrea wasn't too keen on the idea of having her probation officer preach to her. Regardless, it was going to happen. Mr. Bones changed the subject, "So... how have things been going since we met last?"

"Good."

"Why do you kids always respond the same way?... Define good for me, Andrea. Have you been attending all of your classes? Staying away from drugs? Getting good grades?"

"I've been doing better, Mr. Bones. I'm not perfect, but I'm getting there."

"Andrea, I'm not going to make any bones about this. Every time you step foot in my office, you tell me you're doing better, but when I break it down and ask one question at a time, I find out nothing has changed. What's improved since your last court date?"

The sly teen smirked, "I've got a boyfriend now."

Mr. Bones had to admit, that was a cute answer. However, it wasn't exactly what he was referring to. He smirked but didn't utter a word.

Andrea got the point, "I haven't tested positive for drugs for three weeks. Isn't that an improvement?"

"It is," Mr. Bones said. "So, I guess you have at least one thing going for you. Are you working on anything else?"

"I want to be a better person," Andrea told him. "But it's going to take time."

"You've been on probation for nine months, Andrea. How much longer is it going to take?"

The teen shrugged. "I'll get it together. Don't worry about it."

Unfortunately, the girl's attitude was far from unique. Mr. Bones saw it day in and day out — young people with no willpower to improve their circumstances. Sadly, many times the parents of his clients were just as bad.

"I'm going to give you an assignment, Andrea. Between now and the time of our next meeting, I want you to write me a three-page report on the effects marijuana has on the teenage brain."

"What?"

"You heard me. I expect it to be typed up neatly. Don't plagiarize."

Andrea gave him a smug look before mumbling, "Consider it done."

"Thank you," Mr. Bones said. "You're free to go." With that, Philip walked her out to the lobby just in time to see Billy coming in. "Come on back, Billy."

Mr. Bones had asked him to drop by for a reason. "Bud, I've seen some improvement in you over the last few days. What's going on?"

"Is that a bad thing?"

"No, but I'm hoping you can tell me your secret. Something I can use with some other clients."

Billy grinned at receiving such a warm compliment, "I really don't know what's going on, Mr. Bones. I just been spending a lot of time thinking."

"About what?"

"Somethin' you said — 'bout how you care about me and that's why you always be gettin' up in my business all the time. I know this is gonna sound weird and all but I appreciate you carin' enough to jump my case. Sometimes I feel like Momma's so wrapped up in herself that she couldn't care less what happens to me... I guess what I'm saying is I've been trying to do better cause I want you to be proud of me."

Mr. Bones smiled. "I'm glad you realize I care but don't be so quick to judge your mother. Everyone has their own ways of showing love. Just because she's not as strict as I am doesn't mean she doesn't care."

"Yeah, I know. I ain't sayin' she don't care — that ain't what I meant anyway. I'm just sayin' I need somebody like you to lay down the law and hold me to it."

"Billy, you're right. At this point in your life it is what you need. But at the same time, you need to come to the place where you can develop your own sense of what's right and wrong and not require a heavy hand to keep you on the straight and narrow."

"I suppose you're right, Mr. Bones. I'll work on it."

"Atta boy," Mr. Bones said. "Do you have any homework?"

"Yes, sir."

"Go home and get it done. I'll pick you up on my way to church."

Grinning from ear to ear, Billy said, "I'll be ready, sir. You can count on me this time."

"Bring your completed homework with you so I can look it over."

"Aww… Come on, Mr. Bones! Really?"

"Yes, sir. I'm glad you like it when I'm hard on you."

25

Tamara answered the door, looking like she had just woke up. "What you tryin' to do here, Mr. Bones? Steal my son away from me?"

"Excuse me?" Mr. Bones asked. "Billy said I could come by and pick him up for church."

"He's right, Momma," Billy said, walking up behind her.

"Boy, you stay out of this!" Tamara yelled. "Mr. Bones, my boy ain't goin' to church with you or nobody else tonight. He's stayin' here with me!"

"Momma, that ain't right!" Billy shouted back at her.

"Billy," Mr. Bones scolded, "she's your mother and—"

Tamara waved her finger in the probation officer's face, "Don't you start on my son! He's *my* son, Mr. Bones, you got me? He don't belong to the likes of you!"

"She's drunk out of her head, Mr. Bones—"

"I ain't drunk! You just get yourself back to your car and off of my property! You hear me?"

"I'm going with him, Momma!" Billy said, pushing his way past her.

"No, Billy," Mr. Bones interjected. "You need to mind your mother."

Tamara stood on her tip toes and got nose to nose with Mr. Bones. "Are you still ordering my boy around?" Turning to her son, she added, "Billy, you can do whatever you want! You ain't gotta listen to this man!"

"Fine!" Billy yelled, winking at his probation officer. "If I get to decide... I'm going with you, Mr. Bones, whether you like it or not!"

Tamara scowled at Mr. Bones, "How you like crunching on them peanuts?"

Mr. Bones had never heard that phrase before, but he knew what she meant. "I don't know... You told him—"

"I told him he can do whatever he wants to do. Now, don't you try to stop him none!"

"Okay, okay." The probation officer shrugged, "I give up... Who am I to stop him from coming to church. I guess you can come, Billy."

"Yeah, that's what I thought!" Tamara shouted, leaning against the doorpost for support.

Before she could change her mind again, Mr. Bones and Billy headed to the car. "Your mom get plastered like this very often?"

"Happens more and more all the time."

"And you've never told me about it before?"

"Didn't see the point. So, what? You gonna report this to Social Services now?"

"No, Billy. If your mother's not abusing or neglecting you, there's nothing to report."

"Well, she ain't. So, I guess that's settled."

The ride to church was spent discussing the dangers of alcohol and any substances that control the way a person thinks or behaves.

Upon arrival, Mr. Bones had a quick word with Pastor Jahmal, telling him about his invitation to preach at Freedom Baptist.

"I know all about that. Danny and I have been friends for years. He called me up and asked if any of the men in my church might be able to help him out."

"So, you're okay with it?"

"I'm more than okay with it! I'm ecstatic! God didn't save you just to set you on a shelf somewhere, Philip. He wants to use you!"

Billy placed a hand on his probation officer's shoulder, "I'm proud of you too, Mr. Bones."

After church that evening, Mr. Bones drove Billy back to his house, "You wait in the car while I go in and have a word with your mother."

"Please don't, Mr. Bones. It'll only make things worse. Momma already thinks you be triflin'."

"She thinks what?"

"Triflin', man... You know, puttin' your nose where it ain't belong."

"Your mother said that? She's the one who insisted I work with you!"

"I know, but that's Momma for you."

"I'm going to talk to her. You sit tight."

Mr. Bones went to the door and knocked. It took her a while, but Tamara eventually staggered across the floor to answer it. "What you want? Billy's already in bed."

"No, ma'am. Your son is in my car."

"In your car? Why ain't that boy in bed?"

"You insisted I take him to church this evening."

"I did no such thing!"

"Tamara, I was hoping you had sobered up a bit by now."

"I ain't had but two beers all night! What you talkin' 'bout?"

"Billy's coming home with me this evening."

"I ain't givin' my permission for no such thing."

"You don't have to give me permission, ma'am. He's not safe staying here tonight. If you want to report me to the authorities, you go right ahead and do that. They'll take a probation officer's word over a drunken welfare bum's any day. You might even wind up losing custody of your son. Have a good night."

"You can't—"

"Good night, ma'am," Mr. Bones said firmly, shutting the door in her face.

The probation officer attempted to calm down as he walked back to the car. As soon as he opened the door, Billy asked what his momma had to say.

"You're sleeping at my place tonight," Mr. Bones told him.

"Why?"

"Your mother's too wasted to keep an eye on you."

"She's okay with this?"

"She will be. Let's get out of here."

Mr. Bones knew he was taking a huge chance by removing Billy from the house against Tamara's will, but he didn't want her accusing the boy of stealing something and then lighting into him over nothing. Nor did the man want Billy to get away with doing anything he pleased if his momma passed out. What choice did he have?

Just before bedtime, Billy came in and sat next to his probation officer. "Can I ask you somethin'?"

"Yeah, man. What's that?"

"Why you be goin' to church so much?"

"Why do die-hard football fans never miss a game?"

"You sayin' you into church as much as some people be into football?"

Mr. Bones crossed his arms, "I'm a Christian, Billy."

"Don't laugh when I ask this question, but what exactly is a Christian?"

"A Christian is no different than a non-Christian," Mr. Bones replied. "They were born into sin and deserved to spend an eternity in Hell. But they accepted Jesus into their hearts, and as a result of doing that, they'll get to spend an eternity in Heaven with Him."

"Don't Christians got a lot of rules they gotta follow?"

"Don't non-Christians?"

"Yeah, but that ain't what I'm sayin'. I mean, why would somebody want to be a Christian? You know, to always have somebody preaching at you that this is wrong and that's wrong?"

Mr. Bones grinned. At least, if nothing else, he knew the young man was thinking on spiritual matters. "The Lord has made a tremendous change in my heart, Billy. He's helped me realize there's a lot more to this life than I ever knew existed."

"Like what?"

"Like being a blessing to others."

Billy got quiet for a moment. "Wait! You sayin' the reason you be helpin' me is 'cause you got to for the sake of your Christianity?"

"No, sir. I'm doing so because God extended His love to me and now I want to extend my love to you."

"Hmm…," Billy said, "interesting."

An opportunity had arisen. It was time to put the rubber to the road. "So, Billy... from what I'm hearing, you're not a Christian. Am I right?"

Billy nodded slowly.

"Would you like to be?"

"I don't know 'bout all that now."

Mr. Bones watched the young man's eyes. He couldn't tell where Billy's mind was. "There's no pressure, man. I'm not going to twist your arm and try to force you into anything. But if you ever feel the desire to get saved, talk to me. I'd love to show you how."

Billy slumped down on the couch. "What if we do this, then, Mr. Bones? How 'bout you go ahead and show me the scriptures 'bout being saved. I ain't gonna do it right now. I just wanna know how. Then, someday, when I'm ready, I can do it on my own."

"I'd be happy to show you," Mr. Bones said. "Let me get my Bible. I'll be right back."

Mr. Bones was excited for an opportunity to share the gospel. There was a reason Billy came to his house that night. He just knew it. Less than a minute later, he opened his Bible and showed Billy God's plan of salvation.

"And that's all there is to it? Just believin' and callin' on His name?" Billy asked.

"That's it. I mean, you might want to apologize to Him for all of the sins you've committed and tell Him you're ready to change and start serving Him. But that thief on the cross didn't have to do anything but say he believed and Jesus told that man he would see him in Paradise that very same day."

"You know what?" Billy said. "If it's that easy, I want to go ahead and accept Jesus into my heart. I ain't never truly prayed before though. I've listened to you but I ain't done it myself. Can you tell me how?"

"It's pretty simple, bud. You don't have to use any fancy words. All you have to do is speak your heart. I'll tell you what. Why don't you let me pray and then you can pray after I finish? How does that sound?"

"Do I gots to pray out loud?"

"You don't have to, but I would appreciate it if you did."

"Okay... I can do that."

"Alright, let's get down here on our knees."

The two knelt on the floor in front of the couch. "Heavenly Father, we know you can work all things for the good of those who love you. I was annoyed earlier today with some of the things that went on at this young man's house. But now I understand it all. It was for Your divine purpose. Father, I thank You for working on Billy's heart, and I ask You to make this milestone of his life one that he will never forget. I pray that You will give him the right words to speak, that You will soften his heart, and that You will save his wretched soul. I ask all of this in Jesus's name, Amen."

Mr. Bones tapped Billy's back, "Your turn, my man."

The fourteen-year-old tensed up, took a deep breath and began his prayer. "Dear God, I know I been sinnin' and sinnin' my whole life." A tear trickled down his cheek. "I done went and ignored Your rules. I done terrible things. I done told lies and stole a bunch of stuff. I talk back to my momma all the time. I be skippin' school and doin' drugs. Lord, I've made a mess out of my life." With more tears pouring down his face, Billy sniffled a few times. "I now realize You created me. I guess I've always known that part. But I never understood about how You gave Jesus up to die for me. Honest, Lord... I didn't get it. But I'm thankful You gave up Your son for me and that You loved me even through all of the wicked things I be doin'. God, I'm sorry for the ways I been livin'. Will you forgive me and save me? I want to be in Your family."

Billy turned and looked at his probation officer.

"Are you finished?" Mr. Bones asked.

The boy nodded.

"Just say, 'I ask this in the name of Jesus, Amen.'"

Billy repeated him before giving Mr. Bones an enormous bear hug.

"Billy, you and I are now a part of the same family — the family of God."

26

After dropping Billy off at school, Mr. Bones stopped in to see Tamara. She didn't remember a thing from the night before.

"I think Billy must've run off again. Ain't seen him since yesterday afternoon," she said.

It wasn't going to be an easy conversation, but she needed to hear the truth. "Tamara, would you mind having a seat? I think we need to talk."

Tamara appeared concerned, "Is Billy okay?"

"Your son's fine."

Tamara plopped down on the couch, and Mr. Bones took a seat across from her. "Tamara, I love Billy to death. You know that, right?"

"I know you care about him... So do I."

"Tamara, let me tell you about yesterday. You're going to have to listen with an open mind."

Tamara seemed suspicious, "Okay?" she said, dragging out the word for effect.

The probation officer told her about Billy's strong desire to go to church and about how she behaved when he came by to pick up her son.

Tamara seemed shocked, "I don't remember any of that," she said.

"That's what alcohol does. The Bible says strong drink has the ability to deceive. Tamara, sometimes people drink so much that they lose control of who they are, they hurt people, and have no memory of doing anything wrong. I'm a probation officer; I work in the courthouse and see and hear stories all of the time about people who go to prison for murder without even remembering committing the crime."

"I ain't like those people," Tamara said in a soft-spoken voice.

"That's the problem with alcoholics," Mr. Bones told her. "They fail to realize they have a problem until it's too late... Tamara, I came over here because I care about Billy and I'm concerned about his future."

Tamara went on the defensive, "I take good care of my son."

"Ma'am," Mr. Bones corrected her, "when I brought Billy back from church last night, you thought he was already sleeping. When I arrived here today, you thought you hadn't seen him since yesterday afternoon. I believe you love him, but you need to admit to yourself that the alcohol is driving a wedge between you and your son."

Tamara shook her head. "This ain't the first time I've heard a lecture like this... I know I drink too much and I've tried to stop, Mr. Bones... but I can't do it."

"What have you done to try to quit?"

"I've poured it all down the toilet, quit buyin' it, asked friends to keep me accountable — but nothin' works!"

At least Tamara recognized her addiction — that was the first step on the road to recovery. "What if I told you Billy's future depends on it? Would you try harder?"

"What you mean?"

"If you look at statistics, you'll see that boys who grow up without father-figures in their lives are extremely likely to get involved in criminal activity. Those who get into alcohol are even more likely. The other night, you told me you saw nothing wrong with Billy sneaking out and drinking past curfew. That's because you do it yourself and don't want to feel like a hypocrite for telling him not to, am I right?"

Tamara nodded her head, "I ain't gonna lie about it."

"Good... Billy is following in your footsteps. You're his momma. He's going to do what he sees you doing. Show him you're strong enough to put that bottle down... Can you do that?"

"I told you, Mr. Bones, I would if I could. But it ain't as easy as it sounds."

"If I get you some information on a local support group, would you at least give them a call and consider attending meetings?"

"I'll think about it but I ain't promisin' nothin'."

"That's all I ask," Mr. Bones said.

The front door suddenly burst open. It was Billy, "What you doin' here, Mr. Bones?"

"I'm talking to your mother. Why are you not in school?"

"Didn't feel like stickin' around there."

Mr. Bones stood to his feet, "That doesn't cut it with me, Billy!"

"Oh?... Would it be better if I told you there was a bomb threat and they let us out early?"

"If it's true."

"It is," Billy said with a smile. "You can call the school to check. It might even be on the news... You didn't tell Momma 'bout last night, did you?"

Mr. Bones shook his head.

"Tell me what?" Tamara asked.

"Momma..." Billy's smile grew immensely, "I gave my heart to Jesus!"

Tamara leaned forward, "You did what?"

"I asked Jesus into my heart, and He saved me!... Momma, is you saved?"

Tamara shook her head. "I don't know nothin' 'bout bein' saved, boy. I ain't the church-type. You know that."

Billy turned his attention to his probation officer, "Mr. Bones, will you save my momma too?"

Mr. Bones chuckled, "I can't save anybody, Billy. That's something only God can do."

"You know what I mean... can you tell Momma how to get saved?"

"A person has to have a desire to get saved, Billy. We can't just force it on anybody."

"Momma," Billy said, squatting down in front of her. "Momma... look. If I had died yesterday, I would have gone to Hell. But I ain't got to worry 'bout that no more. If I die now, I'll go to Heaven. If something happens to you, I want you to go there with me. Please, Momma... Please get saved like I did. Will you let this man show you how?"

A tear formed in Tamara's eye. "Billy, I've never seen you so passionate about anything in your life."

"I love you, Momma. Please, please do this... It ain't hard. Is it, Mr. B?"

"Mr. Bones," the probation officer corrected him.

"It ain't hard. Is it, Mr. Bones?"

"No. Not at all."

Tamara wiped the tear from her eye. "If it's that easy and you already got saved, why does Mr. Bones have to tell me how to do it? Why can't you tell me?"

Billy shot his probation officer a questioning, pleading look.

"You can do it, Billy. Tell your momma what you did to get saved. You don't have to remember all of the scriptures we looked at. Just tell her what you did and what God did."

Billy took his time and told Tamara everything that had taken place the night before. Before Mr. Bones knew what happened, all three of them were on their knees, and Tamara was giving her life to the Lord. Immediately afterward, she said, "Billy, I've been giving this some thought. I'm going to get sober and I'm gonna stay that way."

"Really, Momma?... Is that what Mr. Bones was here for?"

"He did bring up the subject, but I've been thinking about it for a long time, son."

"That's wonderful, Momma!" Billy gave her a bear hug. "Want me to go in there and dump it all out again?"

"No. I think I'd rather do it myself this time. You can watch me if you want to."

27

Billy held out his palm. "Pay it up," he said.

Mr. Bones reached in his wallet. "Do you know how much money you've earned over these past six weeks?"

"No clue."

"Five hundred and twenty-five bucks."

Billy grinned from ear to ear.

"What do you think you're going to do with all of that loot?"

With wide eyes and a grin that would have lit up outer space, the fourteen-year-old said, "I got me a few ideas."

"Forget about them," Mr. Bones replied.

"Forget 'em? Why's that?"

"Cause your mother and I had an agreement."

"I ain't know nothin' 'bout no agreement? What you talkin' 'bout?"

"That money you earned is going to be donated to a local charity."

"What?" Billy's nostrils flared, "I earned that money! It's mine!"

"Exactly. We've been trying to teach you a lesson through what I refer to as the 'Get What's Coming To You' method. You've seen nothing wrong with stealing people's hard-earned cash and claiming it for your own. Your mother and I thought the best way to break that habit was to have you do some hard work, earn the money, and then have it taken from you."

"That ain't right!"

"Maybe not, but you had it coming."

Billy glared at his probation officer as if he was the cruelest man on earth.

"I do have some good news for you," Mr. Bones said. "You said you love your mother, right?"

"You know I do."

"Do you know what she's been doing today while you've been out here weed-eating this hillside?"

"No. And I don't really care. I just want my money!"

"Your momma's been attending her first alcoholic recovery meeting."

"That's nice," Billy grumbled.

"Billy, that's a big step for her."

"That ain't nothin' compared to givin' no charity over $500."

"I hope this teaches you not to ever take another dime from anybody... You understand me?"

Billy sighed, "You really gonna make me do this?"

"You better believe it! We're going to take this cash down to the recovery group that's helping your mother."

Billy lost his attitude and said, "If we have to give it to somebody, it might as well be them I guess."

"And I have more good news for you."

"I can't hardly wait."

"The guy you split firewood for called me earlier this morning. He offered to hire you for some other projects around his property."

"Why? So you can find an excuse to give away more of what I earned?"

Mr. Bones laughed, "No. This time you're not being made to work. It's your choice. You can accept his offer and keep the money you earn, or you can turn him down."

Billy smiled, "You're serious?"

"Completely."

"He be wantin' me to split more wood?"

"I don't know, bud. From the sounds of it, he has several projects he needs completed; if you prove yourself reliable, they're all yours."

They pulled out of the driveway, and the probation officer's cell rang. "That's probably your momma. Will you answer it for me?"

"Sure."

Billy disguised his voice and answered, "Philip Bones speaking." There was a silence. The teen shot his probation officer a confused look. "No problem... It was the least I could do... Yeah, you too."

Billy hung up the phone. "Why'd you do that, Mr. Bones?"

"Do what?"

"All that cash belonged to you? You been givin' all those people money to pay me for working for them?"

Mr. Bones smiled, "That wasn't your mother, was it?"

"No, it wasn't... You are donating $525 out of your own pocket to the place that's helping my mom?"

"No, you are. You labored for that money."

"But you gave your money to those other people so they would give it back to me. That ain't make no sense!"

"Doesn't it?" Mr. Bones asked.

"I ain't never gonna understand you, Mr. Bones."

28

Philip couldn't have been more pleased with the reports he was getting from Carlos's teachers. That is, until he left Mrs. King's room. He was no more than twenty feet from her door when a boy on the other end of the hallway bolted out of a room, waving his arms high in the air as if he was a monkey – he was clothed in nothing but a pair of whitey-tighties. The kid ran across the hall into another classroom. A few seconds later he was back in the hall and heading toward a third one.

"What on earth?" Philip asked himself out loud.

When the boy came out of the third room, Philip saw his face. "Carlos!... What do you think you're doing?"

Carlos froze in his tracks and erased the smile from his face. "I... uh... Mr. Bones, what are you doing here?"

If there had been any doubt about it before, it was gone now. If Mr. and Mrs. Estrada were on board, Mr. Bones had yet another young man who needed some extra one-on-one time.

A note from the author:

Thank you so much for reading *Redirecting Billy*!
Unfortunately, there are a lot of young men in our society who
are growing up just like Billy. They can be reached if more
people like Philip will take the time to reach out to them. Could
you be one of those people? If you enjoyed this read, would
you mind leaving a review on the site where you purchased it?
It would be a huge help in spreading the word about my books.

Reprogramming Carlos is going
to be a bigger job than Philip
Bones can imagine. To find out
how Philip deals with him, order
Reprogramming Carlos today.